It's anything but a
silent night.

Once Upon a Holiday

USA TODAY BESTSELLING AUTHOR
CLAUDIA BURGOA

Copyright © 2019 by Claudia Burgoa
Cover by: By Hang Le
Edited by: Paulina Burgoa
Marla Esposito
Deaton Author Services

All rights reserved.

By payment of the required fees, you have been granted the non-exclusive, non-transferable right to access and read the text of this e-book on your personal e-reader.

No part of this text may be reproduced, transmitted, downloaded, distributed, decompiled, reverse engineered, stored into or introduced into any information storage and retrieval system and retrieval system, in any form or by any means, whether electronic, photocopying, mechanical or otherwise known or hereinafter invented, without the express written permission of the publisher.

Except by a reviewer who may quote brief passages for review purposes.

This book is a work of fiction. Names, characters, brands, organizations, media, places, events, storylines and incidents are the product of the author's imagination or are used fictitiously.

Any resemblance to any person, living or dead, business establishments, events, locales or any events or occurrences, is purely coincidental.

The author acknowledges the trademarked status and trademark owners of various products, brands, and-or restaurants referenced in this work of fiction, of which have been used without permission. The use of these trademarks is not authorized with or sponsored by the trademark owners.

Sign up for my newsletter *to receive updates about upcoming books and exclusive excerpts.*

www.claudiayburgoa.com

ALSO BY CLAUDIA BURGOA

Standalones
Once Upon a Holiday
Chasing Fireflies
Something Like Hate
Then He Happened
Maybe Later
My One Despair
Knight of Wands
My One Regret
Found
Fervent
Flawed
Until I Fall
Finding My Reason
Christmas in Kentbury

Chaotic Love Duet
Begin with You
Back to You

Unexpected Series
Uncharted
Uncut
Undefeated
Unlike Any Other

Decker the Halls

*For Kristi, I promised you Sterling's story, but it evolved and took a turn —just like life. It's just as beautiful as planned, if not more. Love you.
... and for the mothers who make the impossible to fulfill your dream. I honor you.*

Love never claims, it ever gives. – Mahatma Gandhi

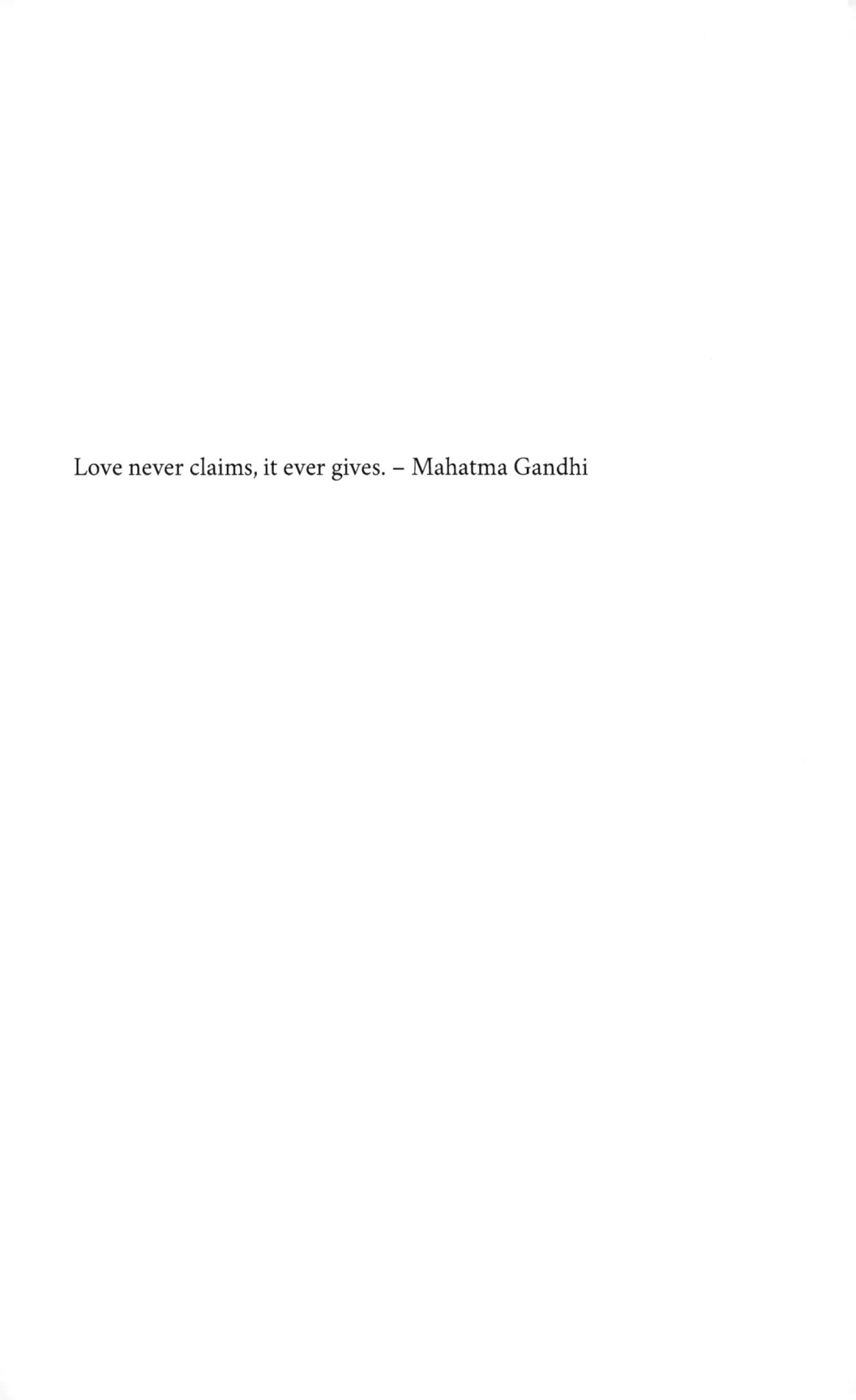

JUNE

You know what to do. Beep, the answering machine blares loudly.

I sigh in frustration. I check the phone number on the website to see that it's correct. Would it have killed them to include a professional greeting?

This better be worth it.

"Good afternoon," I recite calmly into the phone. "I'm calling on behalf of Juniper Communications and PR."

Pausing, I make sure to check the address for the property I found. Multitasking isn't going well today. It'd be so much better if someone could answer the phone so I could get all the information I need beforehand. And on top of all that, there's a long list of tasks I have to do before I begin the next chapter of my life.

Where did this year go?

I feel like November is over and it only started last week. If I blink, it's going to be Thanksgiving and I'm not quite ready yet for what comes next. I scribble the address of the property I just found and make a few notes about the restaurants, grocery stores, and amenities nearby.

Maybe I should search for a gym where I can sign up for a one-month membership. Then, I remember I was leaving a message.

"Right, so we came across one of your properties and would like more details. Could you please call us at your earliest convenience? Thank you and have a wonderful day."

I hang up the phone and take another look at the house online, clicking through each picture. This is perfect for what I have planned. I can't imagine anything more fitting than this as I read through the amenities again. Two-bedroom house with a spacious kitchen and a cozy family room with a built-in fireplace. Only a five-minute walk from shops and restaurants. What better place to take a hiatus while I decompress, relax, and work on my new life?

Now if only they'd call me back so I can lease this sucker.

My cell phone rings a couple of minutes later. I check the caller ID which reads *The Art of Real-State*. Good, at least they're fast at getting back.

"Juniper Communications, how can I help you?"

"Did you just call requesting information about one of our properties?" a husky male voice asks.

And fuck if it isn't sexy. It's powerful and commanding. Not that I like to be ordered around but I could listen to it all day. It's a voice to sink in as it wraps you up. I move my mouse around the screen, bringing back the house in question.

"Yes, that was me."

"May I suggest next time you don't leave a long pause and maybe focus on giving a phone number, a name, and the property you're calling about."

Well, aren't we grouchy today? The hot as fuck voice just lost all my interest.

"Caller ID exists and, obviously, you were able to call back," I explain and continue before he can rant about something else. "Anyway, I'm talking about the house located on Detroit Street. In fact, I filled out the application, but I have a few questions before we can move forward."

"The property is no longer available, thank you for your inquiry," he says and hangs up the phone.

I frown. *What the hell?*

My shoulders slump because the cute house in the middle of the city isn't available. He didn't even let me ask if they had any other properties around the area. What kind of business does this company run?

I could let well enough be but what if the new occupants won't be moving in until January? Maybe *it is* available for the month of December. I just need it for thirty-one days.

"Yo," he answers.

What is he, seventeen? Maybe he's someone's son and he's helping his mom. Nope, that voice belongs to someone older, maybe hotter.

Those hormones I'm taking are making me horny. *Calm down, deep breaths.* He might look like Tommy Lee Jones and not Jake Gyllenhaal.

"Can I speak with a customer service representative or a manager?" *Someone capable?*

"How can I help you?" he asks and by his snippy tone, it's obvious that he's run out of patience.

"Look, I just need a house for the month of December. Do you have anything available around the same area?"

"Maybe?" he answers. "But not for *just a month*."

Okay, so this guy might be some intern and needs a little training. That's fine, I can work with him.

"Would you mind telling me what you have available? My client might be interested if the property and the price are right."

I hear a chuckle and some movement. "What's your email address, sweetheart?"

Promptly, I answer with the general email address, spelling every letter to ensure he doesn't miss it.

"Is that *z* as zebra or *c* as car?"

I tighten the hold of my phone because seriously how can the *c* of communications be *z* as zebra?

"It's *c* as in clown," I reply at his stupid question.

"Got it, lady," he says. "I'll send you a link with the property. You can check it out and send us an email if you have any further questions."

Without saying another word, the fucking asshole hangs up on me. I laugh because if he wants to be difficult, I'll show him difficult. I open the email and click on the link. The house is breathtakingly beautiful. The entrance looks like a tower of a castle. I read the description, *Estate in coveted Old Cherry Hills.*

Well, I definitely don't want an estate. This is huge for little old me.

Eight bedrooms, ten bathrooms, recently remodeled home. Main level gourmet chef's kitchen.

Where else could they have the kitchen? The brands of the appliances are fancy. There's a pool and a guesthouse. Why would I want any of that? *Luxurious master suite features his and her closets, a sitting area and a pristine white marble bathroom with a stand-alone tub and steam shower. Oversized bedrooms with walk-in closets.*

Well, yeah, it's gorgeous and the exterior grounds are marvelous, what with the pool, the hot tub ... why do I want a wine cellar when I won't be able to drink? I tilt my head imagining driving around the circular driveway. Custom built-in bookcases.

This is stunning. If I were to move in there for the rest of my life and have a family ... I sigh because there's so much to do before I can get to the point of having a house full of children.

I read his email one more time but the only thing he sent is the link. There's no information about the monthly rent or if it's available just for one month. So, I call again and there's no answer. Instead of leaving a message I hang up and call again, and again, and again until he answers.

"Did your parents ever teach you how voicemails work?" he

growls. "You leave a detailed message, number, name, and message *after the beep*."

"You don't say," I reply sarcastically. "And then what happens?"

"You wait until the person you're trying to reach calls you back. Dialing the fucking phone twenty times is inconsiderate. I have work to do," he says rudely.

"May I speak with your supervisor?"

"I'm the only person available at the moment, how can I help you, Ms. Juniper Communications? And make it fast because unlike you, I. Am. Busy."

"Are you sure you don't have anything smaller?" I ask calmly. "I don't care if it's in a different area. This house is too big for what we need. It could fit my entire family and we're talking about eight adults and two children. My client is going *alone*. A mansion is overkill. But I'll tell you what, if this is our only option, we're willing to negotiate."

"Excuse me?" he barks the question and if it wasn't rude, I'd admit it makes me hot.

"Actually, what's the price to rent it for only one month?"

"Look, lady, this is the only property that's currently available in the Denver metropolitan area."

"That doesn't answer my other questions. The price and the length of the lease. I just need it for one month."

"Let me be clear, we're not Airbnb." He pauses. "There, I just emailed you the link for their website because it seems that you're looking for a property that you can lease as a hotel. Now, if you like our property on Viking Lane, I recommend you read our company's policies and terms. They are on our website. It's a standard twelve-month lease. We require a two-month deposit and first month's rent. And, in case you're wondering, we don't make any exceptions. Fill out the application online."

He hangs up on me—again.

The stupid voicemail picks up *again* and I'm done with the guy, so I just leave a message. Maybe tomorrow the manager or someone more competent will answer the phone. "We have a very important client who only wants this property for the month of December. Is there a way you can make an exception? We'd be happy to do something for you in return. We are a *public relations* company, after all. Wouldn't you prefer to have free *positive* publicity? You could be leasing this place by the end of January at a higher price just because we used you. We'd like to move forward only if you'd be more amenable to our terms."

If this doesn't work, I'm not sure what I'm going to do. Look for a different doctor here in San Francisco? Nope, this clinic in Denver is one of the best in the nation and they're cheaper. My insurance doesn't cover the procedures.

I call the clinic to confirm my appointment for next week. If I'm lucky, maybe I can see the house and rent it. I only have a month to get everything settled. One month off and if all goes well with the buyer, I'm selling Juniper Communications and …now my phone's ringing. It's the asshole or hopefully someone competent.

"Hello?"

"Look, lady, you seem like a smart person. So, let's be clear. I don't bend shit unless it's in the name of art, not rules. If you're interested, I like to bend beautiful, willing women on a flat surface so I can fuck them hard. I can show you anytime you want. If your client is as important as you presume, I'm sure they could pay the full year without batting an eyelash."

"You should be fired," I complain. "In fact, I'll make sure to leave a poor review on your website. What's your name?"

"Have a good day, lady."

The fucking nerve, seriously, who does he think he is?

JUNE

You know that distracted friend who trips gracefully, loses her shit more often than not, and yet seems to be well put together?

In my circle of friends, that's me, Juniper Spearman.

Not to push some dirt on said friend, but if she's anything like me she's far from perfect.

Let's focus on me. People think I have my life together, but I just fake it. They think they can count on reliable June. Because June knows everything. (I have Google at the tip of my fingers if I don't). She's always ready. (Not really, I just carry everything in case I have to use it.)

Ha!

What they don't know is that I'm just your average thirty-three-year-old.

There's no magic, tricks, or secrets to my so-called life.

Seriously, the side no one sees is so much different.

Then add the list of mishaps I have to deal with every single day. There's not a dull moment when people are around me. And I use my anecdotes as a way to keep my family in the loop and yet away from what's really happening to me.

"We already told you everything about our new place," Jeannette, my twin sister says, taking her phone back.

She just showed me the house she and her wife, Teagan, bought a month ago—in *Hawaii*. I wish I had something as cool as that or the pictures of my three-month-long honeymoon like them. I only have work stories.

"What's happening with you?"

This is already weird. Jeannette and I were super close. We used to have a great twin connection and called each other every day. Last year, things between her and Teagan got serious. So now I'm an afterthought. Which is okay but weird—and lonely.

My life is going through a big change too but I'm not ready to tell her or my brothers so I use my latest tale to keep my life from her.

"So, check this out," I say. "At the airport I had one of those, you grabbed the wrong luggage moments. It was an accident—not my accident though. The couple in front of me grabbed *my bag*. It's okay, I get it. Everyone has a black rolling bag. Everyone."

"You don't have it marked?" Jeannette asks surprised.

I roll my eyes. "Of course, I do, can you not interrupt? So, I'm waiting for it and I'm already searching for my ticket because for sure I thought it'd be on its way back to Toronto. It wasn't until this lady screamed, 'These aren't mine. Whose underwear is this, Leopold?'"

I lift my napkin waving it the same way the lady from the airport did with my stuff as I continue my story. "This woman flaunts my favorite pair of lacy black panties like an enemy flag for everyone to see it. Needless to say, the entire flight from Toronto to Denver plus the airport employees had their attention toward this lady—and my intimates."

Jeannette and Teagan are already laughing at this point.

"You'd think that's the worst part. But it's not," I continue. "I cleared my throat, walked with my chin up and shoulders back to her and said, "Those are mine.""

"So, everyone at the airport saw your underwear?" Teagan asks to clarify. "I would die if that happened to me."

I almost died, but I smile, nod, and continue, "And to be honest, I should've phrased that sentence better, saying something like, *that's my bag.*"

"Oh-oh, what happened?" Jeannette asks. Her eyes are already lightening up because she can feel there's something worse and much more funny coming up.

"The next thing I know she's opening the cosmetic bag where I have my *toys* and shows my pink rabbit thruster, saying, 'So, you and my husband played with your toys. Is this what you like, Leo. Play with brainless twinkies?'

"Turning to look at poor old Leopold who might be Dad's age I said, "next time grab the right bag, man." Without missing a step, I put my things back into my bag. Looked at the agent and said. "There's nothing perishable inside unless you include my edible lube. Would you mind if I leave?" The FTA agent nodded and waved toward the exit. Talk about doing the walk of shame."

"Only you, June." Jeannette laughs as I finish my story. Her wife is choking with laughter.

Thankfully, it's only us tonight. Sadly, she's going to be telling this to our three brothers. I can see how things will unfold. Jackson, the oldest, will judge me silently after laughing hard, because June, the baby of the family, shouldn't be having sex—or sex toys. Then, Alex will be asking stupid questions to embarrass me. Jason will squeeze my hand and take the heat away from me.

"Leopold's wife sounds like a bitch," Jeannette says.

"Yep, I should've left the vibrator with her," I agree, finishing my drink. "Leopold might not know how to show her a good time and that's why she's bitter."

After I finish my story, we go quiet. I look around the restaurant trying to find a new story or something to talk about.

We're at Diego's Steak House. One of our favorite restaurants in Denver. Every time we're visiting our brothers, we make sure to have a meal or two in here. Usually, I'd be having a great time. But this is considered okayish at best.

Jeannette brought Teagan along. Don't get me wrong, I like Teag, but since they got married Jay and I don't spend as much time together as we used to. Would it kill her to give me a couple of hours of her time?

I miss our twin time. This is exactly why she's out of the loop on what's happening to me. If and when she complains I'll remind her of the dozens of times she's cut our phone conversations short and of today.

Before I can come up with something new, they both look at each other, then Teag flags the waiter.

"We should head out," Jeannette informs me.

See what I'm talking about? They're a unit. No more June and Jeannette share a glance and make a plan. The twin connection is gone and so is happy hour whenever we're together. I'm thrilled that she found her other half but I'm starting to feel left out.

Lonely.

"If you two will excuse me, I have to use the ladies' room," I say, and point at my empty glass. "Can you ask for another martini for the road?"

"High altitude," Jeannette warns me. "Two more and you'll be showing your favorite pair of panties to the entire restaurant—and this time you won't be able to claim it was an accident."

She cackles and I think she's the drunk one of the two of us.

"Bitch," I growl and march to the bathroom thinking about how I'm going to get back at her.

I swear she's so loud, a few tables around us hear her and give me *the look*. Maybe I should tell her wife some embarrassing stories from when we were young. There're plenty of those. That might keep them around for a couple of hours—at least one more hour. It's too early to go back to the hotel.

On my way to the restroom, I try to come up with the best one. Then pull out my phone to see if I have any old pictures. I don't pay much attention when I enter the restroom, put away my phone, and enter the stall. After I'm done and while I'm washing my hands, I know exactly how Jeannette is going to pay for what she just did.

"Well, this is either a treat or the worst invasion of my privacy."

I jump and shriek. My heart beats fast but I spin around toward the unexpected male voice. I'm not sure where I should concentrate my attention, his handsome face or the thick and meaty treat he's holding in his hand.

Yummy, talk about girth and length.

"Wait, what are you doing in the ladies' room?"

He laughs while putting away his well-endowed package. "I didn't know they had urinals in the ladies' room."

"In the what?" I shriek and look around the bathroom.

And fuck if this isn't worse than the airport. It's Jeannette's fault. She distracted me.

"Oh, well," I say, smiling. "I'll leave you with your..."

"You should show me something to make up for what just happened," he says, with a hinting tone. "You know a tit for tat."

"What?" I cover my boobs. "No."

"Come on, at least show me those lacy panties everyone saw at the airport."

"How do you know about my panties?"

"You and your sister don't know the definition of inside voice," he says and my cheeks heat up. Well, I gave a show to the entire restaurant. "At least, I think she's your sister. You two could be twins, you know."

"We *are* twins," I clarify. "And, no, I won't be showing you anything."

He winks at me. "You liked what you saw, we could have a party with him as long as you're willing to share."

I don't have time to respond, as my phone buzzes, I take it out of my purse.

Jeannette: *Hey, we're heading out. I already paid the bill. Are you sure you're staying at the hotel?*

Wow, she's abandoning me. I get it, it's cold and she has to drive to Jackson's while I just need to walk a block to get to where I'm staying for tonight.

June: *Yes, please don't tell anyone I'm already here.*

Jeannette: *You owe me.*

June: *Love you!*

Is it wrong to avoid my family for one night?

I'm not in the mood to deal with my brothers and their significant others, yet. We have an entire week to bond and be thankful for … What am I even thankful for this year?

Ugh, who cares. Mom, that's who gives a shit about what we say before we eat. She is going to ask around the table and if possible, she'll make us give an entire speech about it.

I love her dearly but she can be intense during the holidays. I'll think about that tomorrow. I have a couple of days.

What I need today is … I look up and take a good look at Mr. Hot Package. He looks a little like Scott Eastwood with a few extra grays on his sideburns and stubble.

I need someone like …

Him?

"What are you doing?" he asks a little hesitant, almost wanting to snatch my phone.

"Telling my sister goodbye?" I ask, hoping that this clues him in to what we can do for the rest of the night.

Do I really want to do him? I mean, he seems to have the whole package and what a great way to finish this chapter of my life before I write the next one than … this guy.

But we're interrupted by an even taller guy who enters the bathroom, slamming the door against the wall. "What's taking you so long?" He looks at me and says to his wrist, "We have a security breach."

"She's fine. Maybe a little tipsy but nothing to worry about," the hot guy says to whoever just called me a *security breach.*

I take a good look at the hot specimen because maybe I missed something. He could be a celebrity. The real Scott but as I study him, I realize he's no one I know.

"Let's go," the other guy orders.

"Ew, he hasn't washed his hands," I say, scrunching my nose.

They both laugh, but the guy humors me and marches to the sink. I excuse myself and leave. My sister left my jacket with the hostess. I put it on and start walking when I feel someone flanking me. As I glance over, it's the guy from the bathroom.

"Can I help you?"

"Saw you're leaving alone. I wanted to make sure you get to your destination in one piece."

"This city is safe," I inform him in case he's from out of town. "But thank you for the offer. Where's your babysitter?"

He laughs. "He's not my anything, but that's a good one. You're leaving without paying what you owe me?"

Without turning to look at him and as I enter the hotel I say, "Good night, and for the record, I don't owe you anything. It was too dark to notice *your tiny thing.*"

STERLING

Funny how some things work and life sets a morsel or two of joy down after a shitty storm.

Life has sucked for a few years. Everything around me seems colorless, even sad. My life, if you can still call it that, has lost its spark. It's barely recognizable anymore. I can't even call it my own. Today of all days, I have to pretend to give two shits about the company I co-own with my brother.

Having dinner with some of the executives to celebrate their latest project isn't my idea of a good time or a good anything. I did it for my brother who couldn't be here. He owes me. This is what I get for continuing the family legacy.

Fortunately, I had someone to entertain me. For most of my time I observe the beauty that sits a few tables away from the private room we rented for the occasion. I requested the owner to keep the door open.

The first thing I spot are her slick dark curls. She's facing a woman with the same hair color, just shorter and straight. Her voice is silvery, the tone vivid. She keeps the attention of her friends as she tells one story after another. Actually, a few people who are around, including myself remain focused on her.

Everything she says is funny, if not embarrassing at times. But she chuckles, and gestures while keeping us captivated. She's one of those people who can laugh at themselves and enjoy life. The few times she turns her head around I can see she's beautiful. In fact, she looks a lot like one of the other women.

When she excuses herself to go to the restroom, I'm tempted to follow her. Without thinking twice, I rise from my seat and follow. How can I let the chance to meet someone like her go? She's like a breath of fresh air. Talking about funny situations, she happens to be in the same restroom as I am and fuck if it isn't embarrassing and yet a turn-on that she was there in the middle of the men's room.

When I first see her face, I freeze because fuck, I've never seen someone as beautiful as her.

She's stunning.

The kind of beauty you see in Greek sculptures and inspires art. In fact, I want to head to my studio and draw her.

She's about five seven, maybe five eight with mouthwatering curves and the face of an angel. Big brown eyes framed by long eyelashes. A button nose which tip is slightly turned upward. Full lips and a long neck that makes me want to kiss her and so much more.

When Beckett, my bodyguard, comes to check on me, I'm thankful because I'm too old for one-night stands and too jaded to believe this could work. In no time, she's going to figure out who I am and ask for money or a relationship.

Except, her little line about washing my hands and the indifference turns me on and makes me act recklessly.

Or maybe for the first time in years I'm taking a chance. There might be a different spin to the story. The girl is from out of town, doesn't know me from Adam, and she's sexy as fuck.

So, I walk along with her to the hotel, trying to size her up and see how I can convince her to spend the night with me. She doesn't even acknowledge me for the two long blocks we walk together. After her goodbye, I ignore her dismissal and follow her inside the hotel. Just before she reaches the elevator bank, I catch up to her and say, "This can't possibly be it."

She turns around and glares at me. "Did you forget something?"

"We had a moment," I insist.

"A moment? Me seeing your ..." She glances at my crotch and smiles amused. "That wasn't a moment. It was a mistake on my part."

"Come on," I say, winking at her. "Let's go to the bar. Please, have one drink with me and then you can go back to your room. You owe me that much."

"It was an accident," she insists.

I shrug. "Still, I'm a shy boy and need something to help me settle the embarrassment."

She laughs. Looking at me from head to toe. "You're old enough to survive the blow."

"I'm still a kid on the inside."

She laugh-snorts. It's endearing. "Does that line normally work?"

I smirk at her hoping this charms her. "You tell me? Have I convinced you, yet?"

"Look, I'm not the kind of person who has drinks with strangers and ..."

"This could be the exception," I say. "*I* could be *your* exception. I know you're mine. Let's break that dull routine, forget about tomorrow, and have some fun together."

"Look, as much as sex with ..." She snaps her mouth closed and takes a deep breath.

Well, someone has to tell her to finish her sentences. But that won't be me. This woman might be more complex than I first thought. There's something about her that intrigues me.

She stares at me, quizzically.

I'm in my late thirties; I know women well enough. Not that I understand them, I just know when there's a possibility to make a move. Life is about what you make, the chances you take, and the opportunities you create for yourself. I see a possibility in her—with her. Not sure what it is, but I want us to happen. At least for tonight.

After I wait long enough, I decide it is time to remind her that the clock is ticking. We only have this. One moment.

"Was it a cosmopolitan or a martini?" I ask.

Her eyes open wide in surprise. "You noticed me?"

I shrug. "It's my job to observe beautiful and interesting things. You're what gives the world some color."

She twists her lips looking at me suspiciously. "You're good. We practice our lines on how to charm women often, don't we?"

"Not as often as you think, and I'm being honest. I don't lie," I say, lifting my hand and caressing her delicate face with the back of my fingers.

Sparks fly between us. Electricity flows in my bloodstream from the shock. Her eyes shine. There's something about this woman calling to me, pulling me to her. She's like a piece of clay who wants to be molded by my hands and I'm dying to do just that.

"I haven't done this in a while," she says.

"What is *this*, beautiful?"

She takes a deep breath and says, "Meet a guy, flirt, and ..."

"... And I can make it worth it for you," I offer.

She twists her full lips a couple of times then asks, "A last fling before I settle?"

Releasing her face, I take a step back. "Sweetheart, as much as I'd love to make your fantasies a reality, I can't. Not when you belong to someone else."

She laughs loudly. It's a rich noise. Just like her voice it's sweet and soothing. Such a shame this is as far as we can get.

"Oh, no, I didn't mean it that way," she mumbles once she composes herself and shows me her hands. "See, no rings. I'm single and in the middle of the biggest drought. I'm making some life changes and I won't have time to date or ..."

"Hook up?"

"Dating, getting to know someone and be disappointed after a few outings because we couldn't connect." She scrunches her nose. "It gets old, you know."

"Then, let's make your last time worth it. The best one."

She chuckles. "You're so sure about yourself?"

"Of us," I answer. "We could be perfect."

"Perfect," she repeats, staring at me.

I'm enchanted by her gaze and her voice. Whatever happens tonight might be better than it's been in a long time.

Perhaps I'm pursuing this because it has been so long since I tried to spend the night with a beautiful and smart woman who doesn't fall at my feet because I'm *Sterling fucking Ahern*.

There's more though. It's been a long time since my heart has felt this way, pounding this fast, as I listen to a woman's laugh—desperate to hear more about her. If I had the time or the energy, I'd want to win her over, woo her, and convince her to be mine. But as we stand, we don't have much time left.

I trace the line of her jaw with the back of my finger. She shudders, her lips part. "Let it happen," I say. "Have you ever let yourself live in the moment?"

She sighs, there's fear in her face and yet eagerness. She blinks a couple of times and finally whispers, "I want to, yes, I want it."

I feel like the snake, handing an apple to Eve. Good, beautiful Eve who was bored with her life and wanted something different. See how perfect we are together—for tonight. We both need a break, something special that won't last too long but will be a long lasting memory. Since I want to make it good, memorable, I take a step close to her, and smile.

"Are you sure?" I ask, our noses almost touching; our mouths so close I can taste it already.

She nods.

My lips touch hers. I slide one hand to the nape of her neck, the other on the small of her back and pull her closer to me. I thrust my tongue inside her mouth and flick it against hers. Her hands lace around my neck and our mouths can't get enough of each other. I can just feel what it's going to be like to have her for the night.

Her body feels soft and warm in my arms. This is far beyond the kiss I expected, and it takes long enough for me to remember we're in the lobby of a hotel. In public where people can recognize me. Shit, I'm a moron.

"We can go to my place," I offer between breaths, resting my forehead on top of hers.

"Room, I have a room upstairs," she tells me, grabbing my hand and pulling me into the elevator.

JUNE

This is either the best day of my life or the biggest mistake I've ever made. By the way he kisses me, I want to believe this was the best decision I've made for myself. When we open the door of my hotel room, he takes my hand and drags me to him. He bends his head and my mouth opens automatically for his.

This kiss is just as powerful as the one downstairs. A strike of lightning, the collision of two stars, a supernova being born.

It's exceptional. Bigger than life, bigger than the universe. Never before have I felt sucked into a black hole and charged with the energy of the sun at the same moment.

His lips are soft, firm, commanding, in charge of us.

I clear my throat, breaking the kiss and take off my jacket and look at his body.

"Do we have any rules?"

He smiles at me, shakes his head, and reaches out to my face. "Only to enjoy the moment. Tomorrow we'll be a memory. You'll be the beautiful brunette from Thanksgiving week and …" He shrugs. "Hopefully, I'll make this unforgettable enough you'll remember me."

Placing his hands on my waist, he pulls down my skirt and grins when he finds my leggings. "You're layered up, I like it."

I rise onto the balls of my feet, trace his neck with my jaw, and mumble, "More action less words."

"Don't move," he commands as he begins to undress me slowly. First my turtleneck, then my leggings. He slides down the straps of my black bra and I'm thankful I wore something sexy today.

He unveils my breasts.

"Look at you," he whispers in awe. "You're beautiful."

"What do you have?" I ask, tugging his black shirt.

I open my mouth wide. The sight is quite spectacular. Never before have I seen someone as handsome and sculpted like marble. A sexy mass of muscles and strength.

He's so fucking sexy.

Hesitantly, I touch the lines of his flat stomach, running them down until I unfasten his pants. My mouth waters as I stare at him, at his heavily aroused erection.

I want to touch him, grip him, and suck his engorged head.

It'd be fun to straddle him, but he makes the next move, pulling me into his arms and wrapping them around me. My hands slip around his back.

"Make it unforgettable," I whisper against his lips.

He responds voraciously, kissing me with such an intensity I feel like I'm on fire. We get caught up in the heat. He pulls me onto the bed, lowering himself over me. I feel the hot wisp of his breath against my throat. I shiver with pleasure as he nibbles my skin. First along my neck, then my tits.

I push my hips up, seeking some friction, a way to relieve the ache between my legs but nothing works. His mouth is at my breast. His tongue tracing circles until the tip hardens. He repeats the same with my other one. He begins to lap faster and tug harder until I start moaning.

"Please," I beg and I'm not even sure what I want, for him to bring me to my knees or to have him inside.

I grip his shoulders when his fingers tease along the insides of my thighs, padding his way up to the middle of my body where he moves the thin fabric of my panties. I cry out and lift my hips when his thumb caresses my slit.

With ease and expertise, he lowers my panties with his teeth and then pushes them down the rest of the way with his hand.

"Are you sure you want this?" he asks just as I'm on the edge and about to fall into a powerful orgasm.

"You're cruel," I protest. "Of course, I want it, I want everything."

He flashes me an assured smile as he moves his body back up and spreads my legs wider. One second his face is between my legs and the next his tongue slides over my clit, slippery, wet, long, and hot. Every nerve in my body awakens. He does it again, pressing hard and moving slowly. The feeling is too much, overwhelming and wonderful.

This guy knows what he's doing. It's all too much. His mouth, his fingers, his wild lips sucking me. Those teeth nibbling me. And the tongue sliding from my clit all the way to my back hole. My blood runs hot, my cells vibrate with pleasure. I'm tied into knots. I can't think.

I'm weak. Desperate. The thundering of my heart matching the rhythm of his mouth. My lids become heavy, I'm so close, I can feel it. I want him inside. But before I can speak, everything goes dark for a second, it's the prelude before the entire universe explodes and the sparks illuminate the horizon.

"I need you," I say and I'm not even sure where those three words came from, but I feel them.

I feel it.

The desire to have him inside, for him to claim my body.

It scares me for a second because I've never said those words to a man before—ever, and I don't even know his name. I was just letting the pleasure take me wherever it needed to go.

This guy doesn't lose momentum, his body covers mine, his

eyes find mine. His smile, those bright green eyes. Something about him feels familiar, comfortable. His kisses though, they're possessive and this one is erotically arousing as I can taste myself.

Pleasure surges and buzzes with each flick of his tongue inside my mouth. I gasp when he stops and moves away from me.

I watch him roll the condom down his length and then, he's over me again. His lips at my tits. One of his knees opening mine. Pushing himself up, his mouth finds mine, and my body goes still when I feel him pressing himself slowly against my entrance.

The way his thickness fills me, easing himself slowly makes me tremble. I clutch his shoulders, my nails denting his skin. He's too big and the deeper he goes the more I want.

He moves gently, pulling out slowly, thrusting just at the same pace. It's a different rhythm, erotic, even sexy. The same way he kisses me. I want this fast and lift my hips, urging speed. I want it harder, faster. He doesn't budge, with one hand he pins my hip down.

"I want this to last, relax, feel it. This is the first of the night. Let the pleasure flow through your veins, let me lead."

So I let him take me the way he wants. It's different and I never thought I'd enjoy it the way I do. The sweet thrusting pushes me to the highest place I've ever climbed and then in one instant I erupt like a volcano filled with hot lava, melting in him. He rides my orgasm and now plunges himself faster and harder until he finds his release and moans.

He collapses, his chin resting on my shoulder. "I could be doing this forever."

"Me?"

"Worshiping you," he mumbles.

He moves away from me and I whimper at his absence. What is wrong with me? He comes back in bed a few minutes later and tucks me into his side. He traces lines with his fingers and says, "You're a beautiful piece of art."

I don't understand the line and before I can ask, I feel his mouth against mine. I relax, he's not leaving yet. We have all night. Whatever happens tomorrow doesn't matter.

STERLING

It's around four in the morning when I wake up to the feel of *her* next to me. I smile at the sight of the beautiful woman who shared one of the best nights I've had in a long time. If not, the best night of my life.

A part of me wants to break the only rule I set and ask for her name. I could take the jet and visit her often. The way her body molds to mine. She let me possess her, take control of the night. Still, she demanded a lot from me.

How could we fit so well when we don't know each other?

She's just perfect, and fuck if I don't need her touch. I can feel happiness running through her blood. If I needed an antidote to my fucked-up life, I'd drink her whole and keep her with me.

This feeling inside me is so much different. She's like a blue sky. She's sunlight. The laughter of a baby. A masterpiece.

I haven't fucked or kissed this much in one night since … I can't remember. She's nothing like any other woman I've ever met. Let alone had in bed. She's like heroin. You want to shoot it through your veins and hope it stays forever. Thank fuck, I learned fast that drugs only last for a few moments. The high leaves fast and the despair increases.

How bad would it be to change our dynamic and stay with her the entire week? I ask myself as I watch her. Her head rests on my bicep, her long hair tied into a braid—courtesy of the little blow job fantasy. Fuck, she took me deep and swallowed every drop. I wonder if she'll let me fuck her pretty ass. God, I bet she's an ass virgin and I fucking want to take that for myself.

Make her mine, I repeat for the thousandth time since we decided to take this step. That's not the way I operate. She can't be mine. She's destined for someone else. A guy who's waiting for her and will make her happy.

But why not me?

Why does this thing between us feel so right when I know it's impossible?

Her eyes flutter open, she smiles at me. "You're awake."

"And so are you," I mumble, kissing her swollen lips. "How are you feeling?"

"Is it time to think already?"

"Not if you don't want to."

She smiles at me, and fuck if I don't want to be inside her again. I can't get enough of her, her lines and curves. Last night wasn't enough to get to know her body. I want to know it so well that I can sculpt it by memory after I leave her. Carve a version of her that I can keep for eternity.

"I don't want this to end yet," she whispers and pushes herself slightly and hooks her arms around my neck. "Kiss me."

I don't hesitate and kiss her. We fit so well; it doesn't take much for us to melt into one.

"You with me?" she asks.

"Always," I mumble, taking her mouth and moving inside of her, thrusting and pulling slowly. Enjoying the last time and the feel of something so perfect as ... fuck. My blood freezes but I can't stop plunging inside her.

What the fuck did I just do?

Broke the number one rule, but it feels like the best mistake I've done in my entire life.

June

I WAKE UP CONFUSED, happy, and yeah satisfied. Everything during the night felt like a dream. When I look to the side, the bed is empty. It was bound to happen, yet my heart clenches at the thought of never seeing him again.

Except, the guy sits by the window, thoughtful.

Last night was ... actually, when I thought things could never be better, he proved me wrong and this morning it was beyond my wildest dreams.

This was magical—and unexpected. Still, when I see his face, I feel inadequate. I'm not sure what to say. No names, no numbers.

No second moments.

It started and it ended in one night.

But what if?

"We got carried away last night," he mentions.

"Carried away?" I ask.

"You don't happen to be on the pill, do you?"

I can't help but laugh. If only he knew. "No, but I wouldn't worry about it."

His expression doesn't change.

"Look, I'm clean and the possibility of conceiving a child after what happened today is low. Condoms are only eighty-five percent effective, what I have is ninety percent. There would be no consequences."

It's a dream of mine to be a mother, but he doesn't need to know about my hopes, the misery I live, and my next chapter.

He runs a hand through his hair and sighs. "Good, I just. This isn't—"

"Are you clean? Because that's something that I need to know," I interrupt him.

He nods. "It's the first time I've lost my head and didn't use a condom. You?"

I nod and yawn.

"Go back to sleep," he suggests and moves toward me. "I'll keep an eye on you."

Will he be here when I wake up?

JUNE

When I wake up, the guy is gone. A part of me is disappointed because we had an extraordinary night.

Unforgettable.

I stretch, push myself out of bed and smile when I find a note and a few origami flowers made from the hotel notepad on my nightstand.

Thank you for this night.

I recall the heat in his kiss. How alive I felt in his arms. The feeling disappears fast when I remember the guy doesn't fit into my plans. This was perfect, I feel refreshed and relaxed.

Who knew casual sex was so liberating?

No names, no commitments, no expectations. This was the perfect ending to my old life and the beginning of a new one. Next year everything is going to change.

"You got this, June!"

I pack my things, check my phone, and make sure I have the address for the house I'm looking at today. And surprise, surprise. The asshole who manages the company cancels on me via text.

Unknown: *We have to cancel the showing of the house on Viking Lane. There's no one available to meet you this week.*

I call the company's phone number and the stupid voicemail picks up right away and I leave a message. "How can you be in business when you're so unreliable? If I don't see the house, I won't lease it. Find someone to show it to me."

Disappointed, I drive by the house to make sure it's not the money pit and looks exactly how the videos and pictures showed. At least, from the outside. The place is beautiful, even when some of the greenery is dead because winter is coming. There's more to the house than just a mansion, it's a place—a fairy tale waiting for a happy ending to happen.

The possibilities of what I can do with it during the holidays are endless. I can hire a company to decorate it with twinkle lights. Not just the house but all the evergreens that surround it. If I'm lucky, it might snow enough that I can have a white Christmas. Maybe I can stay here for the entire year—the doctor said things might not work the first time around.

When I arrive at Jackson's house, Emmeline, his wife, is the only one there.

"Where is everyone?" I ask.

"Your brothers and your dad went fishing, they'll be back tonight. They have some crazy schedule to follow." She rolls her eyes. "On Thursday they are running a marathon, in case you want to go along. Your mom went to buy a few things we're missing."

I assume that Eileen, Jason's wife, is with him. It's a relief not to have Jackson asking me about my life, my company, and my plans as I enter the house. He thinks that as the big brother he should know everything.

It's also refreshing not to have Alex ask me about *his* life the moment he spots me. That's the problem with being his agent and sister. Jason is the only one who doesn't put me through a thorough interview every time he sees me.

"Where are Jeannette and Teagan?"

She frowns. "Their plane doesn't arrive until tomorrow."

Bitch, seriously? I had dinner with her last night. Liar. I grab my phone and text her.

June: *You owe me.*
Jeannette: *Why?*
June: *You're not at Jackson's.*
Jeannette: *Fuck, weren't you staying at the hotel?*
June: *For one night.*
Jeannette: *Can we be even?*
June: *How long are you hiding from them?*
Jeannette: *I said I'd arrive tomorrow at four?*
June: *You definitely owe me.*
Jeannette: *Love you!*

As I'm about to text her, I receive another text from the unknown number.

Unknown: *You can have one month free to make up for today. Let us know how you want to proceed.*

I grin.

"Everything okay?" Em asks as she pours a glass of wine and hands it to me. "It's just the two of us. The girls are taking a nap."

"Yeah, I thought Jeannette was arriving last night," I say casually. "And the management company is offering me a deal. A free month."

"You could stay here," she offers.

"With my brother hovering?" I shake my head. "You're a saint for taking him off our hands."

"How are you feeling?"

I take a deep breath. "Good, I've been taking hormones. My mood swings aren't bad but I'm horny as fuck. It's a process."

A long process because the doctor said that it can happen at the first try or … might take longer.

"Everything will work out," she assures me. "Trust the journey."

And I do because I know what's waiting for me at the end of the path.

"I'm skeptical because it might not happen, and I might have to —" What are my options?

The doorbell interrupts us. She smiles and says, "Hold that thought, let me check who it is. Your brother's gadgets are convenient if not a pain in the ass at times."

She checks her phone and says, "It's your mom. Are you still not telling them?"

I shake my head. "Not yet. You and Hannah are the only ones who know about it."

Hannah, my best friend and next door neighbor, is one of my biggest supporters. Well, her and Emmeline. My family won't learn until the treatment has worked. If I say anything before, they're going to talk me out of it. Don't get them wrong, my family is loving and supportive but not all the time.

"Just remember there're many options and you have to stay positive," she says, walking away. "We can talk about this later."

I take a deep breath and focus on something else because Mom can sense when something is happening to me. She just does.

"Junie Bean!" Mom says when she walks into the house.

"Hey, Mom," I greet her, marching to meet her so I can help her with the sacks she carries.

"Go outside and help Em, I left more things in the trunk."

"Did you buy the entire store again?" I ask and don't wait for the answer. I know it. She bought everything she could because Jack and Em could use stuff in the future.

Like during Armageddon or whatever catastrophe happens from now and until the next time she visits. How does Em feel about Mom? I bet she hates her.

"She's nice," I assure her. "She has good intentions just..."

"I know, and I actually love when she does this kind of thing," she says, smiling. "You're lucky to have her."

"Depends on how you define lucky," I counter.

Mom can be overbearing with me, the baby.

"Look, your life is going to change in ways you can't understand. I know because it's been night and day since the girls came into our life. Your parents make it less stressful when they're around. I'm sure it'd be easier if you had your mom by your side."

"Once it happens, she'll be my first call, for now, I'd rather have her in China, or was it first India and next February Thailand? I can't keep track where they travel anymore."

"Something like that." Em chuckles.

My parents travel a lot and even when they send us their itineraries, I lose track of where they went and where they're going to be. I just know they're always a call away if I need them.

"What's going on, Junie?" Mom asks when I enter the kitchen carrying some of the bags.

"Excuse me?"

"Something is happening to you," she declares.

Call it a mother's instinct but this woman is like a bloodhound. While growing up, we could never sneak out of the house, break curfew, or lie to her in general.

If Mom knows there's trouble, she doesn't let things go until she figures it out. So it's time to use a truth to cover another one.

"Well, I met a guy last night, I just ..." I shrug.

"You don't think he's going to call you?"

I know he won't, but I slump my shoulder and try to look sadder than I feel. It is a little depressing to know sex can be so much better than I've experienced before but it's over.

"He won't," I answer. "We didn't exchange numbers ..." *Or names.*

She gives me that smile that says, it's going to be okay. *You'll find the guy, no need to rush it. You're smart, brilliant, and any guy would be lucky to have you. These days it's harder for you young ones to meet people. I like technology and understand how times change but it's sad that the connections get lost in the Internet.*

She's been giving me that same speech since I turned thirty. I know it by heart. I can recite it in my sleep. Those words haven't done anything but make me feel like I have to just hide how shitty it feels to be lonely—while everyone finds their other half.

"When are you and Dad leaving for India?" I ask, trying to change the conversation.

"Monday," she responds. "We're actually going to Peru."

Em and I shrug. Well, we were way off.

Mom hugs me and says, "But if you need us you're going to call us, right?"

"You don't have to worry about us, we're all adults," I pause, "except Alex. He needs a babysitter."

Mom places her fists on her hips and glares at me. Not sure if she's trying to say, leave your brother alone or I don't believe any of the shit you just said.

"Really, Mom, we'll be okay," I assure her.

"I just have a feeling that you're hiding something from me and I'm giving you space but only for so long."

"You're the best," I declare, hugging her tight. "I'll be fine, I promise."

STERLING

❄

"Where were you on Thanksgiving?" Weston, my brother, asks. "You skipped it again."

I hate holidays, I don't remind him.

I'm not a traditional guy. Mom said I rebel against society's rules and traditions just for the hell of it. But that's not true. I don't give a flying fuck about what people want.

I'm my own person. It was the way my parents raised me. Let Sterling figure out his own shit. We're too busy with other things. Since then, I've lived by my own rules.

My parents didn't realize what they did until it was too late. Bless their hearts. They both died proud of my brother and disappointed in me.

Even when we never agreed about how I lived my life, I loved Mom dearly. She was clueless where I was concerned, but still a nice person. Her priorities never made sense to me.

If she was still among us, she'd be calling me upset because I skipped Thanksgiving. She'd also remind me Christmas is just around the corner. How she'd expect me to go to mass with her.

She'd be sending daily reminders to put aside my work because I have to spend some time with the family.

This year I have some plans. Not for Christmas but for the month of December. Well, I hope last week's one-night stand is willing to spend the next month with me. Beautiful Juniper Spearman. My desire to be with her won over the logic to stay away.

I tried.

The morning after, as I gathered the information from the woman who wanted to lease the house on Viking Lane, I figured out it was the same person. I decided not to meet her.

We said no names, no numbers—only one night. I even threw in a fucking month free to make it up to her. I should let things be and leave her alone.

But, fuck, she's so fucking hot, adorable, and ... I can't stop thinking about her. The best way to spend the holidays is by keeping her company.

Or leaving for Paris and not come back until you forget her. Who will miss you?

The only family I have left is my brother, Wes. He and I are best friends. It's because he knows me well enough that he shouldn't be asking about Thanksgiving.

But here he is, in my studio, about to lecture me.

I'm thirty-seven, dude. Too old to give me shit because I didn't pick up the phone.

I put down the clay with a sigh and ask, "What's happening?"

He runs a hand through his hair. "Abby doesn't want to say anything, but she wants you to spend Christmas with us."

Hmm, interesting. Why is he doing this? I look at him and there it is. That frown says everything. He's doing something he doesn't want to but has to. The man would do anything for his wife. Even nag me.

"Look, Wes—"

"Hear me out," he interrupts. "It's the first year without Mom."

I glare at him. Mom died two years ago, and I never spend the holidays with them—or anyone.

"Lance is turning four on the thirtieth," he explains. "And wouldn't it be nice to spend some time with your favorite nephew—on his birthday?"

"My only nephew," I correct and sigh. "I'll be there for his birthday, but can I think about Christmas? I have a ton of work before my next exhibit. You know, it's in Paris, in February. I could babysit the nephew while the two of you sneak away."

"Just think about *them*, not me."

I nod once but don't respond.

He's using his wife and son who I adore with all my heart. Still, holidays are on my top list of why bother? I never enjoyed them while growing up. My parents always organized charity dinners or some stuffy party to celebrate them.

"Here, Abby and Lance made this for you."

I pull out the box and it's an Advent calendar. At the end of the year it marks Lance's birthday.

Low blow, Abigail, low blow.

It's colorful and from an artist's perspective, I appreciate the details added by Lance's tiny hands. The boy has talent and I adore him. We can spend hours coloring outside the lines to his mother's dismay.

"Thank you," I say, sounding cheerful. One wrong move and he's going to start lecturing me about my age and how I should think about my future.

Art is all that matters to me.

My near future is a different story. If I can wiggle my way into June Spearman's life for just a few days, I can call this the best holiday season. Still, she's only going to be a brief distraction.

There's nothing more important to me than being in my studio creating new pieces. My next exhibit. I'm married to my work. The only thing that's worth celebrating is when I finish a piece and I'm satisfied with my creation.

Finding a partner and creating a family is at the bottom of my priorities. Actually, it's the last thing I want to have in my present or my future.

Love is too complicated.

Women are pieces of art. Beautiful, interesting, and with soul. It's not only about their outer beauty but what they actually represent when the artist was making them.

The essence of their being.

One has to learn to appreciate them. Love them. If we can't, we have to let them go. There's someone out there who'll know their worth and cherish them.

Commitment and love are hard. There are two kinds of men. The ones who can recognize the worth of a woman and cherish them forever; and guys like me. We're the appetizer. The prelude before someone who deserves them comes along and sweeps them off their feet—like they deserve.

No one believes me but it's true. I tried it once. Be the man who stepped in and tried the courting, flowers, chocolates, and big gestures included.

It didn't work. Fuck, I was told in many words I was a worthless person who wouldn't do much with my life. Kara wasn't much different from my parents.

From a young age I learned to charm the fuck out of a woman, give them an unforgettable night and move on to the next art project.

Except, Juniper Spearman makes me want to stay for seconds and I'm going to do my best to convince her that we can have a few more nights together.

Now, Wes, he's the perfect guy. Dreamy with all those fucking qualities women love. He lives and breathes for his wife. I couldn't. Even if I wanted to. I love change. Why would I want to entertain the notion of something permanent?

I could care less about others. I'm in a continuous state of change. I love chaos.

"Just think about it, okay?" he says, taking the wrapping.

I tap my temple. "You got it, Wes."

He opens his mouth and closes it. "I know it's been a shitty couple of years but ... we miss the old you."

"The last time I checked, I haven't gone anywhere. It's me, just ... different."

"It's okay to miss her. To grieve," he says and gives me a hug before he leaves.

Miss her? I don't miss Mom the way he does. Linda was a different mother to each of us. She always insisted her foster children needed her more than I did because I had everything. I was born an Ahern.

Being an Ahern isn't all that it's cracked up to be. The Ahern DNA will die with me. It's worthless.

JUNE

❄

My chest is tight. My throat feels like it's closing in.

"It's going to be okay," I reassure myself, gripping the steering wheel.

See, this is exactly why I create a routine and follow it. Last-minute surprises give me *the* hives and a bad case of anxiety.

"Breathe right through it, June," I order myself, grasping the wheel even tighter as the car next to me slides so close I think it's going to hit me.

"Bear left," the fucking GPS says.

"You fucking bear left, bitch!" I yell back.

Can't she see I'm having trouble navigating while the snowflakes hit my windshield hard?

Who in the world says they're beautiful and unique? People who don't have to drive under these shitty conditions.

At least, I didn't do something stupid like driving from San Francisco to Colorado. Though, I should've taken a Lyft and not a rental from the airport.

"I've driven around before," I said.

"This should be easy," I assured myself.

"*The house is just a twenty-five-minute drive according to the website,*" I concluded.

Everything I said and thought was wrong. I swear the management company is going to hear from me. If I ever figure out who owns it I'm going to hire a hitman.

Big fail, June. Next time shoot for a place where they have warmer weather. Nothing lower than seventy-two degrees Fahrenheit.

Whose fault is this? I blame my brothers. Jackson and Jason. Maybe even Jeannette. They started this whole let's all be happy movement. It was better when we were all single and heartbroken.

What happened to, *we Spearmans suck at love*?

Everything started with my older brother Jackson. The asshole who hated relationships suddenly found the love of his life. Not only that, he dared to marry and have twin girls. What happened to loyalty and we're never going to find happiness?

At first, it was fine because well, I had my other siblings. But then Jason finds his perfect half.

Assholes!

Just four months ago, Jeannette calls me from Fiji. She married Teagan, her girlfriend.

Bitch, she deserted me.

If Alex finds anyone before I do, I'll kill him.

Deep breaths, June. Killing isn't on the agenda.

Stupid hormones are making me moody. I have to remind myself why I'm here, to find your groove—like Stella did back in that 90s movie. It's the holidays. My favorite time of the year. It's all about Christmas trees, mistletoe, and Christmas music.

But wouldn't it be better if I could share it with someone else?

I should be happy just with myself. That's why I'm doing what I'm doing—on my own. Still, there's something missing, I feel it in my gut and it's been worse for the past couple of weeks. That empty space in my soul grows wider and I don't know how to fill it.

Why am I not enough for anyone?

Every guy I've dated breaks up with me with the typical line, "It's not you, it's me."

These idiots shouldn't make me feel inadequate but when the majority is saying you're wrong, I can't help but doubt myself. I might have my own business but if anything happens to me tomorrow, no one is going to care. Well, my family but that's all.

Now, I can have what I need. A family. No man required. Just an anonymous donor.

Next Tuesday, I'm going to the doctor to get knocked up. This time next year, I'll be celebrating my baby's first Christmas. Who knows, if I'm lucky enough I might have twins or not.

I'm getting ahead of myself. With polycystic ovarian syndrome, I might have trouble with artificial insemination. I'm prepared for anything, in vitro or adoption. The plan is set up and the wheels are turning. I'm selling my company next year and dedicating my life to creating a family. Unless I die of hypothermia.

It's bitterly cold and the snow is falling heavily. Thick swirling snowflakes blocking the windshield. Two lights ago, I almost hit a semi because the brakes weren't responding. According to my GPS app, I should be at the house in a few minutes. Just a couple of turns and I won't be getting out of the rental until … spring?

I can do it. All the amazing delivery services will be at the tip of my fingers. Do they deliver under this awful weather?

How long is this shit weather going to last?

And fuck, I'm not ready for the storm. I'm wearing a hoodie, and the denim jacket I brought with me won't be enough. The plan to visit the mall to buy a cute jacket from Burberry is canceled until next summer.

"In one hundred feet, turn left," the lady who obviously doesn't understand I don't have a measuring tape says.

Someone should reconfigure the way the GPS system works. Specifically, how they give directions. How about turn left at the next block? Next light, in two lights? Three blocks. I can see that, measure that. Miles, feet ... it doesn't make sense and only feeds my anxiety.

Costa Rica, that would've been a better place to go to, it's warmer and no one will find me there. How about Australia? I should've researched fertility clinics in warmer weather or wait until the summer.

Once I park the car, I pull out my tablet to make sure I'm in the right place. With all the snow, I barely recognize the place. Then I switch to my list of important things I want to achieve during the next thirty days.

I check the email the management company sent with the instructions about the keys. I should've asked him to mail them, but this sounded so much easier. There are no instructions.

It says, *see you when you arrive, June.* Maybe someone is waiting for me or the keys are somewhere around the pot or the welcome mat. I should just check. If they're not there, I'll call him.

I leave the car running, grab my phone, and lock the door in case someone walks by and drives away with my things. No one answers the doorbell. I wave to the security camera, in case someone is watching but nothing.

Well, I guess I'll call him from inside the car. However, I realize my stupidity. The keys are inside and I locked it. I try the app to unlock it from my phone but it's not responding.

I call the guy.

The voicemail picks up. "Hey, I'm not sure what we agreed on but I'm outside the house, it's cold and my car is locked. If you could please come by to drop the keys or send help, I'd appreciate it."

I'm tempted to call Jackson or Jason but my stupid phone dies right at that moment. Okay, this isn't working out. Day one is a failure.

STERLING

❄

I'M TAKING MY LATEST SCULPTURE OUT OF THE OVEN, WHEN I notice Beckett standing by the door.

"What's happening, big guy?"

"The camera caught a car arriving at the rental," he explains, and I smile. "The woman was waving at one of the security cameras."

She's here.

I head toward my bathroom and say, "Give me five minutes to shower and change."

"Why don't you let me handle this?" he argues—again. "She might know who you are and want something else. We've been through these same fucking situations multiple times."

No, we haven't done this in a long time. Actually, every time I hook up with someone who fakes not knowing who I am things go fuck ways. Juniper Spearman has no idea who I am, and she isn't impressed by celebrities. She's related to Olympic medalist and X-game sensation Alex Spearman and has worked for several athletes and celebrities. I know her brothers. She wouldn't be like the others.

"She's a professional, I can spend some time with her and not worry about some crazy woman parading at my house wearing a wedding dress like last time," I assure him. "It'll be fun, let me be, big guy."

Fun isn't exactly what I'm looking for. It's more like her company and answers. I have to figure out what is it about June that keeps me awake at night drawing her and trying to remember every curve, scar, birthmark, and line of her body.

Her eyes are brown with golden flecks and I need to see them again to get them just right. Her hair and the way her locks spill on top of my pillow. What the fuck is wrong with me? I don't think about women, in fact, I barely remember anything about them after we spend a night together.

With her … I can't seem to get ahold of my fucking self.

Once I'm dressed, I run a hand through my damp hair and put on my parka, my hat, and gloves. As we step outside the studio, I say, "It's late and I'm not sure if we'll be able to help her with the furniture."

"You know the rules," he says, sternly.

"It's fine, she doesn't know who I am," I say, brushing him away.

If I can help it, she's staying with me tonight. We can either get a room or go to my house. We're definitely reminiscing about what we did in that hotel room.

He sighs. "It's fucking hard to keep you safe when you do shit like this. Hire a real management company to handle your properties."

"Give me the keys," he orders. "I'll drop you and do it afterward."

Jesus, I never liked when my parents controlled my whereabouts and yet, I have to deal with this shit every fucking day. Don't get me wrong, Beck and his team are great but who likes to have a shadow all day long?

Their presence reminds me I'm lonely and that my life sucks.

"Nothing is going to happen to me," I protest and jump inside the car. Before I close the door I say, "Drive."

"If this becomes another shit show, I quit," he warns me.

Which one is he talking about?

My life is a clusterfuck. Being famous isn't what it's cracked up to be. It was all fun and shit when I started. Now, it's a fucking nightmare. I blame all the publications that set me on lists where I became a target.

Like the most influential people in the world. Most successful under forty. Also, I made it to some list called world's wealthiest and most eligible bachelors and bachelorettes. I wasn't some starving artist like the world imagined.

I am Sterling fucking Ahern.

Half owner of Ahern Enterprises. Beautiful women began to parade around the gallery. Thousands of emails and actual letters arrived daily. I'm not exaggerating, there were thousands of those fuckers at the post office waiting for me.

They forced me to buy another property where I could set up my studio. My employees were being harassed too. I sigh, look out the window, and wonder when my life will go back to normal. Hate used to be a strong word but now, I hate so many things and it's so fucking hard to find joy in anything I do.

That's why I have a security team. They stopped the insanity. It's been a couple of years without incidents, thank fuck. The first scary stalker I had terrified the fuck out of me. It was an online threat. A guy wanted me dead because his girlfriend thought I was hotter and richer than him.

The second was a woman named Stephanie who would leave food, letters, mixed CDs, and her underwear at the gallery or my house. There was Gladys, the woman who threatened to cut off my dick if I continued dating other women. She broke into Mom's house—thankfully, my mother was out of town when this happened.

Maggie, the one who brought a kid claiming all her four children were mine almost killed me for cheating on her.

The list is longer than I care for.

When I check my phone, I find a message from June. My blood goes cold when I hear her message. I try to call her back, but her voicemail picks up right away.

"Can you go faster?" I ask Beck. "She's out in the cold."

"Nope, there's a storm. I'm going as fast as I can. Call 9-1-1," he suggests. "Or wait for five minutes. It won't take long."

Exactly four minutes and twenty-seven seconds later—I was counting—the car comes to a complete stop. I look forward, looking at the rental. One of the properties I flipped a couple of years back when I thought real estate was fun.

"There's a car in the driveway," Beck announces. "And I think she's by the door. You better hurry before she freezes."

"June," I call to her, but she doesn't move. I squat and lift her chin. She's shivering and looks sleepy. "It's cold, why don't we go inside."

"It's not cold," she says with a shaky voice.

I look down to try to assess her. She's shivering, arms crossed, and red nose. Her eyes are closed and there might be a tint of blue on her skin. I push the snow beside her with my foot and take a seat freezing my ass. "How long have you been waiting for me?"

"Forever," she yawns, her head resting on my shoulder. Her low voice barely audible. "I was giving up ... thought of you, you know. That it'd be nice if you came to rescue me. I forgot my keys in the car and locked it."

Holy fuck, how long has she been here in the cold? I take off my coat, dust some of the snow accumulating on her head and back, and cover her with it.

"Hey, open your beautiful eyes," I say, moving slightly so I can slide my arm under her legs before I pick her up from the floor. "Please don't go to sleep."

Her eyes flutter open. "But it's nice when I dream of you. Five more minutes."

I try not to freak out but fuck. Maybe I should take her to the hospital.

She sighs and there's another big shiver. I pull her closer to me and she mumbles. "You smell good. Just like I remember. It's funny, I was coming to fix my life and I might not make it. It's sad because I won't leave anything worth remembering."

Oh, fuck, she's delirious.

Beckett has the back door open and I slide us inside. I ask Beck to get her purse.

"The car is locked," he informs me, "and too fucking cold to play MacGyver."

"She's freezing, maybe we should take her to the hospital," I suggest.

He looks at her, takes her pulse, and shakes his head. Then, he walks to the trunk and brings a few blankets. "Take her shoes off, anything that's wet and wrap her with these blankets. Make sure to keep her warm. Once we arrive at your house get her in bed and don't leave her until she's warm."

❄

WHEN WE ARRIVE HOME, I follow Beck's instructions. My favorite is skin to skin, that will warm her up faster.

"How are you feeling?" I ask.

She looks at me as I'm undressing her. "What are you doing?"

"You were out in the cold long enough to get hypothermia, I'm trying to warm you up," I explain, taking off my shirt and my pants.

"Where am I?"

"My apartment," I answer.

"Wait, no, I was waiting for the asshole from the management company. He never arrived."

I get into bed next to her and bring her closer to me. She's so fucking cold, I swear I'm shivering just by touching her.

"Seriously, what are you doing?" she asks, getting closer to me.

I pull her even closer and begin to rub her arms and back with my hands. Jesus, what would've happened if I didn't arrive when I did? I want to kiss her though, I resist. This isn't the time for that but ... fuck, I have the urge to be inside her to make sure she's with me.

Suddenly she's crying and sobbing. I can't make sense of what she's saying. Something about not seeing her family again and how she has nothing.

"Then, I kept seeing these beautiful children. A little boy and two cute girls ... they're so real but so far away."

"Hey, everything is fine," I promise her. "You're safe and I'm going to take care of you. Tomorrow, everything will look different."

STERLING

Unlike many, I don't sleep much. My mind is always busy. I like to draw at night to keep myself busy. Last night was different. Once June was warm enough, I fell asleep, with her in my arms. There's something about the way her body molds against mine that gives me a sense of peace and calm.

What is it about her that makes me act differently?

So different that I had to break the only rule I have with hookups—and between us. No names, no repeats.

How am I going to explain to her how I found her? Talking about stalkers, I just behaved like one but it wasn't my intention whatsoever.

I tried to forget her, to push away the urgent desire to seek her. But how can I when our time together was unforgettable? I needed to see her again—have her again. It was a great night, but we are different people. She seems like the kind of woman who is attached to her family and wants a future. I only care about … what do I even care about?

In the morning, she remains nestled between my arms. I talk

myself out of waking her up with a kiss and trying to seduce her. She's gorgeous and just waking up next to her is a treat and a temptation.

Why are you so special, gorgeous?

She confuses the fuck out of me. It's not the lust; but the wish of remaining by her side. I want to wake up next to her every morning and being able to just slide inside her.

Can I make it happen?

Maybe, once we have a long discussion and we settle things between us. I'll propose a new arrangement. But what if she says, fuck you or worse; I want more from you—or any man who wants to be with me. My head is about to explode with so many questions. Never in my life have I put so much thought into something other than my art, let alone someone.

Pushing away all this madness, I decide to start my day. Before I head to the gym, I leave a note on the nightstand.

Good morning, beautiful.

There're some clothes on top of the credenza. Feel free to take a shower. Make sure to set the temperature to warm. I'm still concerned about last night. Come downstairs when you're ready. I'll have breakfast waiting.

SA

Since the blizzard continues and I can't get her flowers, I make a few flowers with paper and leave them on the nightstand. Again, what the fuck is wrong with me?

I turn toward my bed and admire June. There's nothing wrong with her. She's just perfect and hopefully mine for the rest of the year.

※

June

I can't decide if it was the best dream of my entire life, a nightmare, or if it was some kind of hallucination. My head pounds and I'm hoping yesterday didn't happen and I'm still in my apartment running late.

Lying to myself for a few more minutes only works for so long, but can anyone blame me?

I thought I was going to die. This bed makes me feel like I've landed in heaven.

The scent of the sheets and the softness is inviting.

When I have the strength to open my eyes, I realize the room is dark, the sheets are softer than mine, and the familiar scent of cedar, citrus, and musk. It is sexy and definitely not mine.

Where am I and what happened?

Going through yesterday's events, I remember exactly what happened. I went to the office, made sure my staff knew how to contact me and delegated my tasks. I flew to Denver, it's freezing cold, and ... I almost died.

All because I locked the car and my phone's battery was drained. Did someone rescue me?

Not a smart move, Juniper Spearman. You were a few minutes away from dying. The cold had seemed mild at first. I prayed the management company would arrive soon. Until my face and hands felt numb. Next thing I knew the bitter cold had spread across my skin.

I haven't prayed in my life so hard for a miracle—and it's not even Christmas. Then, there was that dream with the little kids. A boy and two girls.

To add to my madness, the guy I slept with during Thanksgiving week was there too. It felt as if he came to my rescue.

I smell the pillow next to me and it smells like him. Either it's Thanksgiving week or I'm in the twilight zone. I have no idea where I am. What in the world happened to me? Why am I just wearing my panties and a T-shirt? A shirt that just like the entire room smells like him.

My heart races fast because I really can't remember much from last night other than my dreams. Those cute little babies were just adorable. I touch my belly and smile because in just a couple of days one of those kids might be growing inside me but wouldn't it be wonderful if they're at least twins?

Either way, I'm hoping for a Christmas miracle.

Dreaming about my future sounds amazing but I stop myself because I've no idea where I'm at and if I'm safe. I push myself up and sit on the bed trying to see if I recognize the place, but I don't. There's a note on the nightstand.

I read it a couple of times. Who is *SA* and since when do I go home with strangers?

There's no phone in the room. I look around and other than guy's clothing in the closet it doesn't have any personal items. Do color pencils and charcoals count?

Taking a shower sounds like a good idea. I lock the bedroom's door from the inside while I try to find something around that tells me who owns this place.

I don't find anything. It's like whoever owns it is an art aficionado. When I enter the bathroom, I'm impressed. The shower alone has a panel with more than a hundred options where I can regulate the water temperature, pressure, and direction. There's even a massage option.

This isn't my finest moment. Nothing will top this shit. Not that anyone will find out what happened to me. Nope.

I can hear Alex saying, "Remember that time Junie almost froze to death trying to avoid us?"

He can be so irritating. I hate when he calls me Junie. As if he's much older. We're only eleven months apart.

After I'm done showering, I turn off the water, grab a towel, and step out on the mat. The floors feel warm. My body isn't numb anymore, actually, I feel rested.

I finally take a better look at the luxurious bathroom. The white and black tile on the walls is elegant. Very classy. The shower is huge. I could practice barre or yoga before a shower if I wanted to.

I step into the bedroom and look at the clothes *SA* left on the credenza. The sweats and the long-sleeve T-shirt are a few sizes bigger than mine but they're warm and comfortable. There's also a pair of fuzzy socks. They're soft and will do the job to warm my feet.

After I dress, the masculine scent becomes stronger. Whatever fragrance *SA* uses is rich, sexy, and sensual. Musk, cedar wood, a hint of sandalwood, and … something else. I hug the clothes, feeling different. Warmer that's for sure.

They remind me so much of … my eyes widen when I spot a set of origami flowers laying on the nightstand. It's the same guy from that night, but how?

My pulse accelerates. Not sure if it's sheer panic because I can't remember last night or anxiety because I'm seeing him again.

Going back into the bathroom, I find a brush inside the drawers and a hairdryer. This guy is ready for visitors because there're baby products too. My heart skips a beat as I think about babies and children. They are the reason my heart is breaking and I'm not thinking straight.

God, what was I thinking yesterday?

Once I'm mentally prepared to face *him*, I need to know how I arrived here and what happened to me. This is worse than getting drunk and why am I not anxious and worried?

I head downstairs but stop in the middle of the staircase when I spot *him*. He's in the living room. One hand holding a phone and the other combing his hair as he paces. Taking a better look at him, I realize it wasn't a dream. The guy rescued me last night.

He's still hot as fuck. His brown hair is tousled and in need of a good haircut. His green eyes find mine and he grins at me. That smirk steals my breath away and makes my heart skip a beat.

The entire night we spent together replays inside my head. His searing kisses, the way his hands touched me. I had no idea I've missed him. But I definitely want a repeat, not that I should. I'm not even sure why I have all these unknown emotions suddenly sprouting.

It was supposed to be just a once in a lifetime thing between us. Why is he back in my life? And why am I here?

JUNE

❄

"I'll call you later," he says to whoever is on the other side of the line and swipes the screen before he speaks to me. "How are you feeling?"

His voice is low, rough, and it slides through my ears like a smooth bourbon. I could use a repeat of that night, but it won't happen. It's better if I stay away from him. Focusing on the now, I ask some of the questions I have.

"Where am I, and how did I get here?"

He takes a deep breath. "You were sitting on the porch of my rental house, freezing, and I'd say hallucinating. Almost unconscious. I brought you here to make sure you were okay."

"You undressed me!" I accuse him.

He lifts his arms in surrender. "Just to warm you up, my bodyguard who is a former Navy SEAL and a paramedic knows what to do in cases of hypothermia and I just followed his instructions. Nothing happened though, if that's what you're asking."

I'm pissed at him and myself. "Why not take me to the nearest hospital?"

He points to a large window that takes over the entire wall.

We're definitely in a building but I can't see much outside, other than the big snowflakes falling down.

"It's still snowing," I say the obvious.

"Because of the blizzard," he answers. "We were closer to my penthouse than any hospital. It was the logical thing to do."

I have the feeling that there's more to what he wants to say but I let it go. Because there're a lot more questions I need to ask. Like … "How did you know where to find me?"

He exhales loudly. "I own the house you're renting—and the Art of Real-State." He smirks. "I had no idea when I first met you. Coincidentally, the next morning your background check arrived, and I realized you were the same person."

"You canceled," I interrupt. "You fucking asshole. I wanted to see the house and you … you're unprofessional."

"I gave you a free month." He smirks and I hate that it's so charming I can't keep the anger at bay. "Listen, I thought it'd be best not to see each other. I wanted to keep things simple and … obviously I couldn't. That's why I sent you the email saying see you tomorrow. As soon as I was done with work, I went to meet you, and on my way to the house, I got your voicemail."

He walks toward the kitchen which is big and too equipped for a single guy. What if he's … I look at the socks I'm wearing. They're clearly women's socks. I should leave, I have a feeling that staying here any longer is going to end up in disaster.

"Here," he says, marching back to the bottom of the staircase and offering me a mug. "It's Earl Grey tea. I only drink coffee but have some bags in case my brother and sister-in-law visit."

I look at the socks and lift one foot. "Hers?"

"Part of her Christmas present. They're new and now yours," he clarifies.

Okay, so he's not married. *June, don't get any ideas. He's hot but stay away from him.* With a sigh, I go all the way downstairs and grab the mug. I take a sip of the tea. It's not too hot or too cold. It's bitter but not as much as black coffee.

When I look up at him, I wonder what I should do and most of all, how did I get myself into this mess? I'm not going to stay at his house. Not after finding out he owns it. I'll demand my money back. But then what am I supposed to do?

"This is a disaster," I confess. "Nothing has gone as planned, you know."

"Planning is overrated," he says casually.

"What are you talking about? The only way to make sure everything works properly is by planning. If not, look at what happens."

He laughs. Even when his laugh is throaty, rich, and so hot that my body becomes too aware of him, I frown.

Control your urges, Juniper!

"You're one of those," he declares, and he sounds somehow disappointed. "How many journals do you have? I bet you use different calendars and color code every item on your list. Just like your clothes, meals, and activities. Well, planning didn't work, did it? You almost froze."

My ears heat up and I glare at him. "You don't know me," I protest.

He doesn't understand that if I didn't orchestrate my life, everything would be a string of disasters. Didn't he listen to my airport story a couple of weeks ago?

"Tell me I'm wrong," he challenges me.

"It's so not the point," I argue because he won't know why I do what I do. "We just met. So, what if I plan every minute of my day? Having a routine and knowing what to expect is helpful."

He laughs again. "That's not living."

"Says you, because you're what, an expert on life? The Dalai Lama of Colorado so to speak?"

He smirks. "No, but I know him. D and I are on the same level." He winks at me. "He's cool, you know. Not uptight. He'd tell you to chill and learn to experience life, not to structure it."

"In those words? Ha!" I roll my eyes.

He shakes his head. "He doesn't speak much, but I learned from him to enjoy the moment and learn to appreciate what I have."

It's not possible, is it? To know the Dalai Lama. I mean. He … who is this guy?

I look around his penthouse. The place is different from any apartment I've ever visited. Seriously, where am I? It's not a bachelor pad, more like the museum of modern art. There's no leather couch, big screen, pool table, or wine fridge filled with beers.

Nope, this one has a long upholstered couch facing a gorgeous fireplace. Oils hanging on the walls, sculptures on stands or just standing because they're big. There's a dog bed, dog toys, and clothes all over the floor. This looks like a mix between a gallery, a bachelor pad, a doghouse, and a teenager's room.

He needs a cleaning crew. Where's the dog?

I get closer to the art on the wall and I discover something interesting. "*Sterling*," I say out loud and turn around.

Okay, so this guy is loaded if he has at least three paintings from the famous artist Sterling. His art is expensive. I've had a couple of clients asking me to get them some specific pieces from this guy and it's almost impossible to get through to his assistant and even when you do, the answer is always the same, "*Check the website. Only those pieces are for sale.*"

"You know him?"

I shrug. "Kind of. Not in person. I figure he's some sixty-year-old guy who's swimming in money because his pieces are expensive."

"Never googled him?"

I shake my head. "I have enough with my clients to be dealing with others."

"Others?" he asks, and I look at him.

He's holding a bowl and his left brow is arched. "What does that mean by *others*?"

I wave my hand. "It doesn't matter."

Instead of talking shit about a pompous guy who thinks he's Auguste Rodin or Michelangelo, I decide to change the subject.

"So, when can I occupy the house?" I ask.

He lifts the bowl and says, "Here, have some soup."

"Soup at this time?" I ask, a little confused by his offer. "It's ..."

"Almost noon," he answers. "Lunchtime. Look, I understand this isn't part of your life plan, however, there's not much we can do. Everything is closed."

"Maybe I should just call my brothers, one of them is bound to live close by," I say, not knowing where I am.

"Where do they live?"

I start looking for my phone. "Where is my phone?"

"Beck took it, it was dead and soaking wet," he answers.

Well, how am I supposed to get out of here?

STERLING

❄

"At least eat your soup." I point at the bowl. "When was the last time you ate?"

She takes a seat and her head falls slightly as she slumps her shoulders.

"Umm … my brother Jason lives close to the mountains and Jack owns a house located in one of the ritzy neighborhoods. Actually, it's not too far away from the rental. Like a ten, fifteen-minute drive? It's in what I call Pretty Lane Street."

I can't help but laugh at the description of where her brother lives. She might be uptight but she's still funny.

The cute pout and glare she's giving me make me want to kiss her. Her voice between amusement and anger is just delicious. "Are you laughing at me?"

"Not exactly, but it's kind of funny the way you describe your brother's house. There's no such thing as Pretty Lane Street."

"Well, I call it that because all the houses in the area are beautiful."

Who the hell is this chick?

"The storm is coming down hard. You're safe here and your

brothers are better off staying at home. Once the storm is over, my bodyguard will get your car and you can call your family," I suggest.

She yawns and closes her eyes. "Thank you, this ... I just—"

"Drove in the middle of the storm and you weren't sure what to do when you arrived at the property. It was cold, you were alone and frightened," I finish her sentence. "I'm glad you're here, and that I was able to reach you in time."

She rubs one arm and looks at the table. "That's not what I was going to say but yeah. How do you know I was scared?"

"Because listening to your voice mail terrified the fuck out of me," I answer. "When I found you, I wasn't sure what to do, but I was thankful to have Beck. He knows what to do in case of emergencies. I bet you were a thousand times more."

She twists her lips and asks, "Why would you be scared?"

"Well, you were too cold and unresponsive. For a moment, I thought I might lose you." I take a deep breath because it wasn't a pleasant moment. "It was fucking frightening. I'm guessing when you found yourself alone in the middle of the storm it was *bad*. I wish I had been there sooner."

"You confuse me," she whispers.

"Welcome to my world," I counteract. "It's been like this since … we met. So, what do you say? Stay with me for a few days. At least until the weather calms."

Maybe I can get her out of my system by then. Not sure what she's thinking but I need to know that I might have a chance to have her one last time.

※

June

"You think too much," he says.

Pressing my lips together, I glare at him. He has no idea who I am and he shouldn't assume anything. But he's right, I think too much.

He pushes the bowl closer to me. "At least eat your soup."

My brain says no but my stomach growls so loud the hot guy smirks when he hears it. Can I hate his good-looking face? That charming gaze and those friendly eyes are telling me, relax, we'll have a good time.

Never again. *It was a once in a lifetime, mister.*

I'm pretty sure he offers those happy times to beautiful, sophisticated women often and no one ever sees him again. It was supposed to be that way. Then why am I here? I frown when I remember what he said; he was worried about me—scared.

That's so sweet.

Forget it, June. You don't engage with charming, friendly, smart, rich, and uncommitting men.

"It's just soup," he says. "Not a marriage proposal."

I laugh. He has no idea that soup is the last thing on my mind. I wish I could tell him I'm fine, but I'm starving, I take the spoon and look up at him. "Thank you, I appreciate what you've done for me. Even when you could've arrived a little sooner."

"You never told me when you'd arrive."

I sigh. "Maybe it's in part my fault. I shouldn't have assumed. I had a lot to do before the flight and then the drive from the airport. The only thing that kept me sane was thinking about the cozy fireplace in the master bedroom. Here it's nice but ..."

Finally, I take a spoonful of the chicken noodle soup. It's tasty. Better than canned soup. Did he cook it?

I want to ask if he made it when he asks, "Well, when does the furniture arrive?"

"What?" I ask, not understanding his question.

"When did you schedule the moving company? I assume you were waiting for me and the movers when I found you."

"Movers? No, only the prick ..." I stare at him. "Or you, I guess. Those phone calls weren't pleasant."

"Sorry," he apologizes, "I was in the middle of a project and you kept interrupting me but for some fucking reason, I wanted to hear your voice."

He shrugs and I frown because either I misunderstood him or he thinks I have furniture. "The house is furnished, right?"

"No."

"Yes, it is," I insist.

"No, if you read the contract thoroughly there's no mention of furniture. You don't have …"

I open my mouth wide because that's not what he showed me. "What about the pictures?"

"Staging," he explains. "Once I finished remodeling the place, I hired a staging company, we took the pictures and well, here we are."

My lungs collapse because what am I supposed to do now? I'm not going to furnish a house where I'm only going to live for a month. There's a plan and he's fucking with it.

"Look, we can try to work things out," he says, sitting next to me. "You can stay here."

"I don't know you," I tell him, moving my chair away from him. "So what, now I stay with you for a month?"

Is he insane?

"Well, I was going to suggest that you stay here until the storm is over and we can get you some furniture," he suggests.

"One night, we go on our separate ways," I remind him. "No names, no regrets."

He blinks twice and exhales harshly. "You have a pretty good memory and we're going to have to forget about those words. And fuck if Beck isn't going to kill me."

"Your bodyguard?"

He nods.

"Let's start from the beginning." He extends his hand. "Sterling Ahern, it's nice to meet you."

I open my eyes wide and my mouth falls open too. "Seriously,

Sterling fucking Ahern." I don't know much but I know he charges millions for just a piece of art. Well, that explains why he has his own art around.

"Just Sterling, I keep the *fucking* out of the name for obvious reasons."

"That's a terrible joke," I say and shake his hand. "June, but I guess you know that."

As we touch, the warmth that seared my skin the night we were together is back. I release him immediately because I shouldn't be feeling that way but ... I do. And what does it mean?

"Juniper Spearman," he corrects me, taking my hand back, his voice melting me just a little. Enough to make me want to get closer to him.

He looks at me intensely as if trying not only to read my mind but speak to my soul. Hypnotized by his stare, I begin to talk. "What's bothering you?"

"So far, this trip has been a disaster." I pause, snatch my hand out of his grasp, and finish my soup.

"My future is up in the air and my life doesn't seem to be as easy as usual. It used to be so simple to think ahead, create a plan, and just make it happen."

"You seem like a successful woman, what's not working out for you?"

"My personal life. That's why I took a detour and during this month I'm concentrating on myself. I have a thirty-day plan to reset and restart."

He looks at me amused and I wait for him to release a loud laugh, just the way my brothers would do it. He doesn't.

We stare at each other for a few minutes. Neither one says a word. I wish I knew what he was thinking. This is, after all, a famous man whose success is known throughout the entire world. I'm just a woman who manages people like him. Jeannette says I'm the mediator between the deities and their fans.

"Life isn't what you plan," he says, "but what you live, June."

"Dalai Lama?" I ask.

"Snarky, I like you—a lot. No. That's an Ahern original. Same with never color inside the lines and life is what you make with what you have."

"If I don't have it?"

"Work for it, but enjoy what you have," he counteracts. "Always cherish what you're given or what you've done. Never ignore it trying to pursue what you don't have."

"Quotes of the day calendar?"

He laughs. "Wisdom I've collected while I traveled."

"If I ask for my money back?"

"Why are you here?"

I smirk and as I'm about to answer *because you brought me here,* he interrupts. "In Colorado, not at my house. You're running away from a problem. What's happening?"

"You're assuming again."

He shakes his head. "Juniper, I'm an artist. An observer. I understand human behavior. I also listen." He taps his chin and narrows his gaze.

"It's more like changing my life and rethinking what I'm doing. I hate dating but I want a family. The last guy I went out with … you know I get the typical it's not you it's me but—"

"Possibly," he confirms.

"Ouch, don't sugarcoat it."

"You have the power to choose who you date. If you choose a bunch of losers …"

I smile. "That's a good theory."

Then, I look around and sigh. Staying with him is impossible. I have to leave. There's an attraction between us. We could act on it again

… but what's the point?

"How much do you think it'll cost to buy the furniture?"

"It's seven thousand square feet … a lot of money. We could

furnish it, but I don't think you'll get the furniture delivered soon. It's the weekend and there's the blizzard."

He makes it sound impossible. I'm not familiar with blizzards. The only times they've affected me is when I travel. They either delay or cancel my flights, but days…

"How long will *it* last?"

"Who knows?" he answers. "The weather stations and some websites predicted a three-day blizzard. However, our weather is unforeseeable. The storm can stop right now and that's the end of it—or last longer."

"Where am I supposed to stay?"

"Stay here," Sterling offers again.

I stare at him. *Stay?* and … do what?

STERLING

❄

There's something wrong with me. On second thought, she is what's wrong with me. I'm almost begging her to stay—at least until the storm tapers off.

Never have I ever begged a woman for anything, not even a kiss. So why am I doing this? Because I want to understand my obsession with her. The time I've spent trying to bring her to life in my art.

I doubt it.

Staying close to her isn't what I need. She's who I need. There has to be something I can do for her that'll keep her interested in me.

Stop it, asshole. The next step will be wooing her and trying to convince her to stay. But stay for what?

It's only a month. She leaves in thirty days. There's a longer expiration date than just one night and I'd like to take the extension. Is it possible to get her out of my system after those thirty days?

As I observe her, I know there's something bugging her. A problem she needs to solve soon, but she's not sure if it's possible.

Could I offer my help? Will she accept it?

She seems like the kind of woman who wants to show the world she can do everything on her own, but deep down wants someone to hold her hand. Independent, and scared to accept that she needs others.

I could be him. The one who she can count on while she's going through this change.

"You're a stranger," she speaks.

"But we know enough that you can accept my offer. The guest room is comfortable," I lie because I want her in my bed.

"Tomorrow I'll just take a cab to pick up my car—"

"The one you left running and it's most likely in need of fuel?"

She groans, stands up from her seat, and takes the bowl to the sink where she washes it. Totally type A personality. Too orderly and ready to plan every second of her life without even noticing what's around her—or enjoying what she's built.

Once she's done, she walks toward the fireplace and takes a seat. She pulls her legs toward her body, hugging them and settling her chin on top of her knees.

Her pout is cute. It's refreshing to be around a woman who doesn't care that her curls are all over her face. She's a natural beauty. Big brown eyes, long eyelashes, and her mouth—I just want to taste those full, heart-shaped lips again.

What are you thinking, sweetheart?

"Beckett will take care of your car once the storm is over," I mention. "You could use my computer to order furniture."

"I can't spend money on new furniture," she responds, her gaze on the fire.

"It's on me," I offer. "After you leave, I can increase the rent and make it an executive home."

"Am I expected to rent it for the entire year?"

"That's what the contract says," I remind her because maybe she can come back and we can have another weekend together. "Look,

I'm giving you a hand by buying the furniture. I'll have my lawyer draw an amendment to it."

"Thank you for letting me stay here and I'll take the furniture too." She laughs. "This isn't part of my thirty-day plan."

"Thirty days?" I ask and take a seat close to her. "What's in this plan?"

She shrugs. "You'll think I'm crazy."

"Or I might help you. This season isn't my favorite. I could use a distraction."

"It's on my iPad but it includes things like relaxing, learn calligraphy, pay it forward for an entire day, learn more about my family history—"

"Like genealogy?"

"Yep, Mom says her great-grandmother was Native American, but she doesn't have any proof and then Dad's grandmother had some Irish and Spanish roots. It'd be cool to learn more about them. Take a solo trip, for pleasure. I'm always traveling for work. Though, it's something I'd have to hide from my family. I might just go up to the mountains. It'll be short and just me, you know. Everything I'm doing is top secret."

"Why?"

June explains to me she's the baby of the family. Three older brothers and a twin sister who was born five minutes before her. She talks lovingly about her parents. How her father retired a few years back. Since then, her parents travel all year long except for the holidays. She has two nieces—also twins—and her brother Jason and his wife are expecting a baby.

As she speaks of them, I can feel the love for her family just as I feel the melancholy of what her siblings have, and she doesn't. A family. It can get lonely for some, and more during this time of the year.

Go home and be with them, I want to say.

I also want her to stay with me for the entire month. We could keep each other company and then there's the question of why I even want that when I really don't give two fucks about having someone—except, I care for her.

This isn't what she wants, and I can't offer her more. I can't even fake I would be there for the long run. A month is enough for me but what about her?

Art is all that matters, I remind myself.

I stand up and look down at her. "You're welcome to stay for as long as the storm lasts. The computer is in my office. You can start looking at furniture. We can try to buy a few pieces online and the rest we'll go and purchase once we can go out."

"Thank you," she says. "For listening."

"Make yourself at home." I march to my home-studio, I need to work.

STERLING

❄

I SPEND ALL DAY IN MY STUDIO WORKING ON A FEW DRAWINGS—OF June. Then, at dinnertime I come out and find her cooking. There's never been anyone else cooking for me, let alone a goddess like her. She's wearing just the T-shirt I gave her. I stare at her long legs and imagine them wrapped around my head as I pound my dick inside her.

Dude, change your train of thought or you're going to lose her before you have her.

I try to push down the urge but how can I when she's so fucking beautiful. Her hair is tied into a messy do. Some strands hang around her neck. For one hot second I wish for this to be my life. The next I just want to bend her over the counter and fuck her hard.

"Hey, I hope you don't mind," she says, not taking her eyes away from the cutting board.

How does she know I'm here? I watch her cutting the vegetables meticulously. She has two pots on the stove and a big pan. There's a large plastic bowl right next to the cutting board she's using, and I'm intrigued about what she's cooking.

"You know how to use the knife," I say, impressed by her skills.

She shrugs. "I took a cooking class or two in San Francisco. Cooking for one and impress your date."

"Did you impress anyone?"

She laughs. "I'm kidding. Mom taught me how to cook. She taught the five of us."

"You guys are close?"

"We were closer."

And while she continues cooking, she tells me more about her family. How even when she had Jeannette, she always tried to play with the boys. "Sometimes, they would play tea with us. Other times we played football with them or whatever sport they were practicing. Even hockey."

She finishes dicing the onions and pours oil into the pan. "I hope fajitas is okay with you. I debated between that and stir-fry. I decided that eating Mexican food would help us forget the storm at least for a little while."

"Do you like Mexican food?"

"I love food," she responds. "I'm better at eating than cooking."

"Once the storm lets out, I'll take you to Ene's, it's one of the best Mexican restaurants in town," I announce.

She turns to look at me and her eyes focus on my cheek. She takes the dishtowel, wets it, and cleans my face. "Were you working?"

I nod.

"I like your paintings better than your sculptures."

"So, you know who I am?"

She shakes her head. "I've seen some of your stuff and just googled you while you were working. I had no idea who you were before we ... were together, if that's what you're wondering."

I nod, not sure how to explain how bad it can get when I sleep with one of my fans, even more when they have ulterior motives. "Can I help you with anything?"

"Why don't you change while I finish? I have the feeling that you don't do this often."

I'm about to tell her that I cook often but my phone rings. It's Beckett.

"What's happening?" I answer right away.

"I ran a thorough background check," Beck states.

"Of course you did," I groan and walk away from the kitchen. When I take a look at my clothes, I decide to take a shower. I'm black from the charcoal I used earlier. "Just so you know, she's not some crazed groupie wanting to steal my underwear or wanting to have my babies."

"Her family is well off, she owns—"

"Let me stop you there, big guy, I know about her PR company."

"That she's selling it?"

I open my mouth and close it intrigued by this piece of information. What are you up to, Juniper Spearman?

People intrigue me. Their behavior holds my attention much longer than a good thriller. June is as complicated as my brother Wes. The guy who likes to plan every step of his life but when he fucks up it's beautiful to see him behave—like the rest of us.

How much of herself is she hiding?

"Do you need anything?"

"Nope," I answer automatically. "You and your guys should enjoy your day off."

"I went home, but Clark is in the apartment, in case you need him."

I own the penthouse and the floor below that has two apartments. One of them has my security system while the other houses my security team.

"Okay," I say before hanging up.

When I arrive at my room, the bed is made and the flowers I made her are on top of the nightstand. I'm not sure how we're going to sleep tonight. There's a guest room but I want her to stay in my bed and how is it possible that the thought doesn't scare me?

In fact, I think I have at least a couple of aces under my sleeve to make her stay with me for a little longer. If the storm continues during the weekend, we won't be able to order her furniture until Monday, maybe Tuesday. I can invite her to Steamboat afterward. It's just what she needs, a trip. It's not by herself, but if I can just figure out what that list is about, I can try to stay close enough to help her—and to enjoy her.

After I clean up, I head back in the kitchen where I find her setting the table.

"It's still snowing," she complains, setting down a bowl with refried beans. I look toward the window, lift a shoulder, and walk to the kitchen. "It's lovely in here but I feel trapped. I'm not sure if I could adjust to this weather."

Now, if she asked me how I'd like to spend my blizzard days I'd answer, with you in high heels, a lacy bra, and nothing else. First, I'd take her against the wall or on top of my desk with her legs spread. I could eat her right here in the kitchen.

"Everything okay?" she asks.

I lick my lips and nod.

Nope, I have cabin fever and a hot woman in my house.

"The storm will stop soon, the snow melts fast and in a couple of days it'll be sunny." I open the cabinet where I store the tequila and show it to her. "Do you want some?"

She shakes her head. "I'm abstaining."

"Is that part of your thirty-day project?" I ask, pouring myself a shot.

"No, it's the yearlong project that comes right after."

"Are you looking for the meaning of life?" I ask, helping her set up the table.

"No, just doing or learning things that I might not have time to do later," she responds, deflating a little. "Sounds stupid, doesn't it?"

"Nah, I think everyone should take the time to find themselves. Some do it before they become adults, others take the step at a later age. There's no judgment. Actually, I think it's brave to step out of your comfort zone and change your present. So, any insight on what else is on that list?"

"Thank you, I guess. Get inked, learn to snowboard, binge watch shows I've never watched before, find that friend that will stick with me, date someone who's not my type, write about the good things in life, find those things first." She tosses her head back and laughs hard.

"Let's go to Steamboat this week," I offer.

She bites her lip. "I have a doctor's appointment on Tuesday. Maybe afterward?"

I tense, my heart speeds up with fear. I ask, "Are you okay?"

"Why?"

"Well, you're working on a bucket list and going to the doctor. I don't want to assume but, are you sick?"

"I'm fine. It's something else," she whispers. "It's a long story and I don't feel comfortable sharing it with you."

"Fair enough but if you ever want to talk about it, I'm here," I offer. "I guess, what I want to say is can I help you with the list?"

"Why?"

"Feels like something I can do and why not have that memory."

"Okay," she agrees, and I can hear the uncertainty.

"Are you up for the adventure of a lifetime?"

She smiles and nods. June looks so sure of herself, and for the first time, I feel like I have no fucking idea what I'm doing. Seriously, what the fuck am I doing?

JUNE

Cooking is fun, though, I'm also an expert on takeout. I serve a mean pizza on paper napkins or pad Thai when I work late hours. The taco truck that parks across the street from my office feeds me most mornings with breakfast burritos or afternoons with an order of tacos or just nachos.

Still, the few times I have enough time, I try to prepare my food and next year I have to learn how to be more conscious about what I eat. To start making it a habit, and after stalking Sterling on Google, I decide to spend some time in his gorgeous kitchen. It shocks me that it's not just equipped with state-of-the-art appliances. There's real food everywhere.

What's more surprising is having a man padding barefoot around the kitchen helping me set the table. It's been a long time since I shared a meal with a guy. Not any guy though, Sterling Ahern. Who, by the way, isn't old or ugly either. He stands close to me, with wet rumpled waves falling partially over his forehead. He's handsome and so sure about himself.

Something about his offer has me thinking about the list.

What is it that I want to accomplish?

Then, there's the doctor's appointment. I haven't had my period yet so what if the doctor says I'm not ready?

"Do you think the snow will clear up by Monday?"

"Sure, it's been going on for two days and from here it looks like it's tapering off. If the sun comes out tomorrow, the snow should melt fast and the streets will be almost clear by Monday. Why?"

I glance at the big window and wonder what *almost* clear means.

"I have to go to the lab first thing in the morning for some blood work, to prepare for Tuesday's appointment. Then, I have to do some shopping—and well, the furniture."

He nods, pulls out his phone, and taps it a few times.

"One of the guys will drive you," he announces.

"Babysitters," I say with a hint of mockery.

"Bodyguards," he growls but I can see a smile playing on his lips. "It's not by choice in case you're wondering."

Not by choice? I've worked with athletes and celebrities and not many of them have a security team. What makes him *need* one?

While we finish setting the table, I keep wondering what is real and what is fake about the *artist* he shows to the world. When we sit down to eat, I fire my next question. Hopefully, it's the right one, because he seems like the person who doesn't like to talk much about who he really is.

"How often do you entertain?"

He smiles and takes a forkful of the Spanish rice I made, chews, and takes a sip of water to wash it down. "This is good."

"Thank you, I like rice a lot so don't be surprised if I make a bowl or Greek food tomorrow." I try the rice and he's right. I outdid myself this time. Maybe it was the fact that I had some extra time to prepare it. It never comes out like this. It's usually overcooked.

"What makes you think I entertain often?" He gives me a

dazzling grin. That grin that captivates me and reminds me how good we were together.

A flush climbs up to my hairline as I think about the last time we kissed. The third time we fucked. I stare at his muscled arms trying not to think about the muscles he packs beneath the T-shirt and worn jeans.

Not the best memory to replay as we're trapped in his house for another couple of days. I go back to our current conversation. The best I can do until I can at least check into a hotel is keep things friendly. "The fridge and the pantry are well-stocked. Anyone would think you have a family living here—or at least a roommate."

He prepares himself a taco, and it drives me crazy that he's ignoring me or at least the question.

"So, how often do you invite women to have … dinner with you?"

He regards me with narrowed eyes.

I'm instantly remorseful about my words. "I didn't mean it to sound judgmental."

"I live alone. That's the way I like it. If you're speaking about the guy you googled, I'm not him, but I accept that I had a misspent youth." He exhales loudly. "It's a long time ago. I don't eat out often. Unless you count the events that I have to attend. We have plenty of food because my bodyguards stick around often."

I take a bite of my taco and after I chew and swallow, I say, "Sounds lonely."

He looks at me and appears to consider what I said before he speaks, "It's not."

Sterling drinks some of the tequila. Not like a shot but as if he's drinking bourbon. He leans back and watches me speculatively. I can't help staring at him and for a second, I want to be the person who can convince him that having someone by his side is actually better than how he lives.

"I like my solitude," he speaks. "People are welcome to visit and stay for a while but never to stick around."

"So, no significant other," I conclude.

He snorts. "No, I don't get attached to anyone or anything."

I tilt my head toward the bed and all the paraphernalia he has for his dog, "How about your dog?"

"I foster dogs," he answers annoyed. Clearly, he's not used to being the center of attention and to have someone intruding with so many questions. "I don't have time for a permanent pet, a woman, and not even my family. I'm almost forty and honestly, I like the way I live."

The tone he uses when he speaks makes me wonder if he's trying to convince himself that his life is good or doubting what he's done so far. Maybe it's me. I'm trying to read between the lines because from where I stand, he's a catch.

Wouldn't it be amazing to have him in my life?

But it's obvious that we don't fit. It's not like I want him to fall madly in love with me and propose but … He seems like the kind of guy who cares about others. He reminds me of Dad and my brothers. They'd take off a coat for a stranger and give their lives for their loved ones.

"So, you don't plan on ever getting married and having children," I conclude.

"I don't believe in marriage or having spawns. It's not for me. I'm selfish and to have children you need discipline. Same for a wife. My work consumes every second of my life."

I dig into my rice, trying to think about what he's saying. "Belonging to someone isn't time-consuming. My parents have been together for forty years and they're still crazy in love. They belong to each other and … It's natural to want to be attached to someone."

Not that it's happening to me or that it might ever happen. I stop talking because I can see that no matter how much I argue he doesn't even care about continuing the conversation. Love might not be part of his vocabulary.

"What are you looking for, Juniper?"

The question is so simple and yet, pretty complicated.

"Joy," I answer. "If you're wondering if I'm looking for a man, the answer is no. Love isn't something you seek, I've learned that the hard way. It comes to some; others have to find happiness in other forms. But I'm not waiting for things to happen, I never do."

He nods. "You seem like the kind of woman who takes charge of her own life. Even when fun incidents happen to you. I guess you don't enjoy surprises."

"It depends on what surprises you're talking about." I watch him intently. "There's a huge difference between a surprise party and one of your best employees quitting your firm and stealing your clients. Some believe that life just happens, but I'm a big believer in making things happen."

"You need to live a little more," he murmurs and there's worry etched into his handsome face.

I'm puzzled by the connection between us. It's like we can sense what the other is missing or maybe we're missing some pieces that the other seems to have.

"So, you're telling me you didn't plan on becoming famous?"

"It all started out of spite. My father didn't want to pay for college. *"Art is a hobby,"* he'd say. My parents never believed in me. I had to show them that I could make it on my own."

"Did they pay for anything?"

"Nope, it was part college loans and part my brother sending money afraid I'd end up selling my kidney to cover my rent. New York isn't cheap. I wanted to make it on my own. Nothing would've stopped me. My parents were waiting for me to quit and say, you're right, I can't do anything without your money. Even after his death, my father expected me to take over the company and assume all his responsibilities. I had a lot to prove to them and … to myself. No one believed in my talent."

I want to tell him that it takes a lot of discipline and hard work to become an artist, especially to become *him.*

"Do you believe in yourself?"

He looks at me puzzled and yet as if I have just given him the answer to the meaning of life. Does he understand this is a question?

❋

AFTER DINNER, Sterling and I clean up the kitchen. He invites me to watch a movie in his entertainment room. The penthouse doesn't look like much at first sight but it's huge. I expected a simple family room, no, the place looks like a movie theater. We watch television for the rest of the evening.

Erase that, I watch shows while he is enthralled in his sketchbooks. He goes through several of them. Doesn't crumple them, just goes to the next page. Poor man, I think he lost his muse. Does he even have a muse?

"No inspiration?" I ask when he turns the page over.

"Plenty," he answers, staring at the blank slate. "Never been so inspired in my life. What do you say we call it a night?"

I stretch and nod. "What time is it anyway?"

"Almost midnight," he says, looking at his phone. "Do you want to sleep in my room or the guest room? I'll take whichever you don't."

"What's the difference?"

"The guest room doesn't have a comfortable bed. If I were you, I'd take my bedroom," he offers, and I feel as if there's an ulterior motive to it but I'm afraid to ask.

We leave the entertainment room, head upstairs and he simply says, "Have a good night, June."

He walks away and doesn't look back. What am I missing?

STERLING

On Sunday, after a long sleepless night, I head to the gym. Beckett and Clark, two of my bodyguards, are already working out. We don't say much for a couple of hours but on our way out Beckett asks, "You still plan on going to Steamboat?"

No.

A smart man would stay away from a woman like Juniper Spearman. She's dangerous. A unique subspecies with multiple layers that I'm about to peel. Apparently, Dad was right, I don't use my head. If I did, I'd run the other way.

She makes me want a lot of things, like pushing her against the wall and fucking her until she screams my name. I should fuck her today so I can find peace and make her leave tomorrow.

Who needs a woman like Juniper Spearman?

Yeah, she's cute. Maybe beautiful and tall enough that if I wanted, I'd only have to bend my head slightly to kiss those full, pink lips.

I'm contradicting myself every second of the day.

"No. I think the trip is a waste of time," I answer. "It's better if she leaves as soon as we furnish the house. Make sure that happens no later than Wednesday."

He nods. "Call if you need us."

I salute him and board the elevator. As I enter my place, I take a step back. There're piles of papers on the floor. Who's the messy person now?

After another glance, I realize there's a pattern. I pick up one of the documents and I feel my face scrunching as I read it.

Donor No. B893028 and there's a description of a guy.

"Is this like Tinder for people with OCD?" I ask as I step closer to where she sits. "Or maybe you're matching your DNA instead of your personality?"

"This is a private matter," she says, staring at her notebook and then the piles.

"What are you looking for, a mail-order husband or just their juices?"

"Again, this is private," she says without looking at me.

"Honey, if you want a good time, I can give it to you …" I offer and walk to the kitchen counter where there's even more stuff.

The header of a fertility clinic grabs my attention. I look at it and whistle when I see the cost for each thing listed. Semen, artificial insemination, IVF … "Free of charge," I finish my sentence.

Hey, she's hot and sex with her is fucking amazing. If that's what she wants I'm willing to start a new agreement. Instead of one night, one month. Or we can fuck for as long as she wants. Just, without the baby part. I'd love to fulfill her fantasies. I bet she has never let herself go and had some fun with sex.

I put the paper down though and push away my own fantasies. She wants something serious—too serious. A kid. That's what she's been talking about. Her one-year plan. Well, she might want to rethink it because children take about a lifetime.

A child is a big commitment. I might hate my father—the same way he hated me—but we have so much in common. Neither one of us can love or care for another being. Dear old

Dad was an asshole. I'm just as heartless as him. All these men would be better suited than me. Who the fuck would want my genes?

Her list of thirty things to do in thirty days is also on top of the counter. I cringe when I see: *Do something good for someone.*

Suddenly, shit has gotten real and my blood freezes. "Wait, I thought you said you couldn't have children?"

She finally looks at me, her eyes are red and I'm pretty sure she's been crying.

"It's close to impossible. I was seventeen when the doctor diagnosed me with PCOS. That's polycystic ovarian syndrome," she explains. "He said it wouldn't be impossible, but it'd be hard to have children. The older I get, the harder it is. I've been doing a lot of research and artificial insemination is the first step. I think I have the perfect candidate. I've been taking hormones to ensure that I ovulate. Still, the chances of me getting pregnant with the procedure are low. If the first two treatments don't work, they'll harvest my eggs, fertilize them, and implant them once they're ready."

She gives me a sad smile. "I know it sounds crazy."

Everything she's been saying makes sense. She's searching for what makes her happy. She doesn't sit down on her ass and wait for life to happen. Still, she doesn't enjoy life either.

"Of course not, this explains so much."

"I tried you know," she says, and I frown. "I tried to have a family the conventional way. Mom says the words 'you can't' are my motivation and my downfall."

"What does that mean?"

"Since I was young, I had to show everyone I could do anything. I obsess so much I lose myself inside the projects and lose track of what matters. Hence, I'm taking a couple of years off to try to learn how to balance my career and motherhood."

I grab the piles of documents she has on the floor carefully and set them on the counter. Seems like a cold way to make her dreams come true and yet, I admire her for finding a way to make it happen for herself.

Where do I fit in this project? I'm not sure, but I want to help her create that family. Maybe I can have my security team track these men. They might be anonymous but there's always some paper trail lingering around and my men can figure out if they are who they said in the questionnaire.

"You're not judging me for not having a husband or someone to raise a kid with," she speaks.

"Are you judging yourself for that?"

She shakes her head. "It'd be nice to have someone. I see my two older brothers and my twin sister with their significant others and I want it. Of the five of us, I was the one who couldn't be alone. Since I turned fifteen, I've had a boyfriend. My brothers called me a serial monogamist. I gave up because love seems to elude me. The feeling of loneliness though, that follows me around everywhere."

"Do you think a kid will come to fill the emptiness?"

"No, but this kid would be someone I can love unconditionally, forever. That's all I want to do you know, have a family I can love and care for. I'm done waiting for a guy that will see past my personality."

"Sweetheart, if they can't see how amazing you are, they don't deserve you." I take the papers and go for a bottle of scotch. "Let's make a toast so you can find the right guy to make babies. Well, the right donor. We're going to go through every one of these profiles and find you the right guy."

She looks at me and suddenly she bursts into tears.

"What did I say?"

"What if it doesn't work out?"

I put everything down, take her into my arms, and hug her tightly. Fuck if I don't want to fix everything for her. I lift her chin and brush her lips slightly.

"There are plenty of ways to have a child, a family. You can be a foster parent and you can adopt children; there are so many that need love. Just keep that in mind."

"Single woman, remember?" She points at herself. "I'm not saying it's impossible, but it's harder to get approved to be anything. It's painful enough to be let down by my body. Adding a bunch of bureaucrats will kill me. I couldn't stand to hear that I'm not enough for a kid who needs me just as much as I need them. They'd rather keep the kid in the system than give it to someone like me. I've gotten too many rejections in this life, but I'll keep it in mind."

"Hey, don't cry, we'll make it happen," I assure her. "And you'll be the best fucking mom ever."

Between sobs she says, "I'll just try to be as great as mine. She's amazing. Even with five children, she makes us feel that we're special. We never lacked for attention or love. I'm not asking for five, I just want the one, you know. Or those little kids I imagined when I almost froze."

I move us to the dining table and sit with her on my lap. For a while, I let her cry while I hold her and assure her that everything will be fine.

"Why am I even crying?" she asks, mumbling and sniffing.

JUNE

I WISH I COULD STAY LIKE THIS FOREVER, NESTLED BETWEEN HIS arms. He quiets down all the noise inside my head and makes me forget what I'm missing. If I could, I'd stay here forever, in his lap, my head resting on his chest. Wrapped in a cocoon he's created just for me. His heart beating softly against my ear.

If only I knew why he's in my life. Hannah, my best friend and neighbor, has a theory that life isn't a coincidence. Every event happens for a reason and every person who enters your life has a role in it.

There's even a quote on her website about it that at the moment escapes me. Her point is that when you cross paths with someone, it's because they're part of your journey and they fit just right.

Maybe I should call her and tell her what's happening to me. She might be a few years younger than me but she's so much wiser.

Is she right though?

Why's Sterling part of my journey?

Surprisingly, we fit.

He's like an old friend who walked back into my life after years of not seeing each other. Yet, we just met. This weekend has been perfect. Even energizing. I'm scared of what's to come but also sure that everything will work out perfectly.

His loneliness hurts me more than my own. Because he's resigned to be like this for the rest of his life while I want to find something to fill that space—someone. A baby. Tonight though, tonight I want to tear down the walls I build around myself for him. Let him inside and allow myself to just be.

This time is different from the first one. It's a crazy move, so unlike me but just as I'm about to lean close to him, he does it first. He's looking at me intently, a glint in his eye that makes me squirm and heats me all the way inside.

Sterling presses his forehead against mine and kisses my nose and exhales. "We can't."

"What do you mean?"

"I like you." His voice is low even tortured. "More than *like* you. I've never wanted a woman more than I want you right now—or since that night."

"Then why not?" I ask, gathering my courage and not listening to that little voice that says, *he's right, June.*

"You're ready for a lot more and that's something—"

I press my lips to his and give him a quick kiss. "It's one night, Sterling. You want me just as much as I do you."

"Am I part of your list?" He chuckles.

"Maybe? It's so easy to forget about lists and trying to be perfect when you're around. I'm not sure why. All I know is that it feels so liberating. Why not let me have something I've never had? A night where I can have a fantasy."

His eyes burst into flames. It's as if a beast just woke up with my words. Whatever I said pushes him to the ledge. His hand slides behind the back of my neck, he pulls me even closer before his mouth takes mine.

Sterling's lips are so soft, tender at the beginning but he deepens the kiss right away.

I melt. My heart is about to burst into flames. The urgency of the kiss ties my stomach into knots. I've never been kissed with so much hunger—need. Not even by him. Quivering in his lap, I try to get closer to him even when it's physically impossible.

My heart is pounding fast and hard. So hard I feel like I'm shaking inside. I don't know if I should let him lead or just get naked and ride him. My core is aching with so much need.

"I can never be," he says, gasping for some air.

Putting a finger on top of his lips, I assure him that I understand. "You're an amazing guy, Sterling. A man who gives more than he realizes and tonight I'm not asking for more than having mind-blowing sex with me. The one only *you* can give me."

"Baby, I'll show you how great you are and how amazing this can be."

The stupid nagging voice is reminding me every two seconds to stay focused. It's here now and over. Don't plan, don't imagine, don't believe in stupid dreams just because his hoarse voice is hypnotic and his mouth is magical, I shouldn't want more than tonight.

He picks me up and carries me to his bedroom.

When we arrive at his room, he sets me down on the floor and pulls my sweatshirt over my head. Promptly, his mouth is on my skin, running along my neck. His teeth pulling down the straps of my bra off my shoulders.

I moan as his hands roam around my waist pushing down my leggings.

"What's your fantasy?"

"Hmm?" I moan when his mouth suckles my still clothed nipple.

"In bed, what do you like?"

"I'm not sure, never had mind-blowing sex and I know because so far everything is just okay."

"My little blue sky, that's easy to top and make it perfect. By the end of the night, you might have a fantasy—and I'll fulfill that tomorrow."

He finishes undressing me and undresses himself. He reaches for his nightstand and takes out a condom. A part of me is annoyed because, how many women has he brought here? Then, I remember this is the kind of guy I want for tonight. The player who knows how to please even if it's only for one night.

He places the condom on top of the bed.

"We don't need it, trust me."

His eyes stare into mine. "We can skip it," he says thoughtfully. "It's not the first time we'd do it without one."

"Sterling," I whisper, enthralled by his gaze and trembling in need.

He walks over to me. Grabs me by the waist and bends down to kiss me. One hand on the back of my neck. His long fingers massaging my scalp in a way that makes me shiver. Even that touch feels sexy—erotic.

His lips move against mine. Gentle and loving. The kiss builds in intensity, his tongue slides into my mouth and strokes mine. The pace is painfully slow and yet, delicious. My brain is unable to think much but my body is becoming aware of every stroke of his fingers, his tongue, and his movement. Movements I match, like I know the choreography to this dance.

Which is funny since I've never danced like this before. This is a tango. More like a Lambada. Those dances where body parts touch slowly or fast and it's the preamble to a mind-blowing orgasm.

I let out a loud moan as his rough hand goes over my breast and pinches my nipple. My entire body heats up when his mouth tugs and bites my hardened peaks. One of his hands slides down my belly and reaches between my legs.

His feverish eyes meet mine as his rough finger slides along my clit. That devilish smirk widens as I shiver. His gaze burns with the same desire that's possessing me. He licks and sucks my breasts teasing me. The heat inside me roars like a beast, rising up into my throat and escaping as a cry.

I push my hips toward his hand, needing more and wanting everything. I've never had this kind of need or desperation. The foreplay feels short to what I want in this moment.

"Take me," I order. "Don't play, I want you inside me."

"Sweetheart, the appetizer is what makes this special."

My body is begging for him, not his words. He ignores me and his fingers continue playing along with my slit. Teasing my entrance ... both of them.

I gasp when he touches the more sensitive one.

"Fuck, you need to explore more than missionary, Ms. Spearman."

"Are you going to explore me?" I ask with a throaty voice I've never heard before.

He lowers his head to my breast again. He nibbles the tip, then blows some air and nibbles it again. My back arches and I try to push myself closer to him needing more. A cry escapes me. It's pure wanton. Delight.

I run my hands over his broad shoulders, down his arms until I find his cock. It's just like I remember. My mind returns to our first night together and where his mouth was.

I'm so busy fantasizing about his mouth that when he pushes two fingers inside me and his thumb brushes against my clit, I come undone. It's explosive, hard, breathtaking. My limbs are loose, and my legs are shaking.

He smiles down at me, satisfied.

"Are you sure you want to continue?" The question feels like a warning.

JUNE

Sterling is unexpected. Caring, quiet, and loving.

It's impossible to resist him but I know where we stand. We have a week, maybe a month together before we have to part ways. Maybe I shouldn't have done it without a condom. Then I remember what I've read throughout the years. Miracles can happen but sometimes you have to be prepared to give up the fight and find a new path.

I don't regret using his computer to print the donors or using one of his notebooks. Talking with him about my future helped me. Sunday, we spend time together. I lose track of time and remain on the couch reading. He has a nice collection of classics on his bookshelves. I don't ask if they're for decoration or if he reads them. Actually, I stopped asking deep questions because the more I get to know him the more I like him, and what if I finally end up falling in love with a guy who doesn't have anything to offer?

Thinking about my future has always mattered but now it's essential that I act using my head and not my lust. After dinner, he sits down with me to discuss the pros and cons of some of the donors I've chosen until we find the right one.

By Monday, the sun is shining and as Sterling mentioned, the streets are starting to clear. Of course, there're big piles of snow on the sidewalks. I start the day preparing breakfast and praying that what I order online arrives before I have to go to the lab. Thank goodness I don't have to fast for the blood tests, or I'd famish.

There's some noise coming from the front door, and when I turn toward it, I recognize the man from the restaurant. Beckett, Sterling's bodyguard.

"Good morning, Ms. Spearman," he greets me as he sets the car keys on the counter.

"Morning," I answer, gifting him a smile which he doesn't return.

What did I do?

"Your car is on the private level," he announces. "When you're ready to leave, let me know so I can give you access."

In other words, get the fuck out and never come back.

"She's staying," Sterling says, sauntering into the kitchen. He grabs me by the waist and kisses me deeply. Then, he turns to look at Beckett. "Also, you're driving her around today. The rental is a small sedan and only the main streets appear to have been plowed."

"Ahern." Beckett's voice is gruff, even menacing.

Sterling waves his hand. "It's happening. There's nothing you can do. Actually, there is."

"You got to be fucking kidding me," Beckett says when Sterling hands him over a black card. "We have a protocol and rules. Her best friend co-owns an online magazine."

"How do you know?" I ask, flustered, setting the spatula on the counter and glaring at him. "My family and friends are off-limits."

"I can't have someone like you close to *him*. You can make a lot of money out of this situation."

My blood boils because this asshole has no idea who I am and if

I could I'd punch him, I would. I don't though. Let's get real, he's as solid as a wall of steel.

"I don't need money," I clarify. "I'm not an opportunist. Yes, Hannah co-owns a magazine, but she focuses on self-help and all the new age movements or old-world teachings. She explores them."

"That's her focus. Her magazine has an entertainment and gossip section. You can still be helping her," he insists.

This man is obviously not going to budge, is he? Sorry, Hannah.

"Even if I told Hannah where I am staying, she wouldn't say anything. If you did your homework, you'd know who she is, and she'd be the last person trying to sell anyone's privacy."

Sterling looks at me, then at Beckett and shrugs.

"Interesting," he says. "Beck, make sure to bring her bags up to my bedroom. You're driving her today. This weekend we're going to Steamboat. She needs appropriate clothing for this weather and the trip. Plus, there's that furniture store close to the mall. Make sure to take her there too."

"We have rules," he repeats and I'm wondering if he is human or some advanced AI. "She has to go."

"I agree, we have them for a reason. However, she's my guest."

"*She* is right here and hates when *they* talk about *her* in third person," I protest.

"Please excuse his manners," Sterling apologizes.

"I'd appreciate it if you could take me to the mall." I take charge of the conversation. "I'm not used to driving in these kind of conditions. I'll pay for my own clothes—not the furniture."

"See, *she's* just a guest," Sterling assures him.

"Ugh, my name is June, not she," I argue and say, "There's plenty of food for both of you."

It's a peace offering. I don't want him to leave me stranded in the middle of nowhere starving. I plate the waffles and bacon.

"I already had breakfast," both say at the same time.

"Oh," I say and then take a good look at Sterling who seems ready to head out of the house.

"I work out early, have breakfast, and then go to work. I should be back around nine. Please, make yourself at home," he says dismissively.

"Okay," I answer and I'm not sure exactly why I'm disappointed about his last words and the way he just leaves without giving me a proper goodbye.

※

"How was today?" Sterling asks during dinner.

Against his security team's wishes, he takes me to dinner to a small hole in the wall close to his penthouse. It's called *Like Home*. He explains to me how the menu changes every day and every meal. They have guest chefs every shift. It's lovely and cozy.

"We got all the furniture, but it won't arrive until next week," I answer, taking a full spoon of pumpkin soup.

"The tests?"

I sigh. "They drained all my blood. Tomorrow is the appointment. If everything goes well, next time this year I'll be buying an ornament that says, baby's first Christmas."

He smiles and squeezes my hand. "That'll be my present to you."

"I thought you don't celebrate the holidays."

"I don't but it seems like an important gift. If you allow it, I'd like to be around. Become the godfather or something."

"I'd like that."

Sterling smiles. "Would you mind if I go with you tomorrow?"

He's such a considerate guy and a good friend. I wish he could see what I see in him. If I could give him a little of what he has given me in just a few days.

※

June: *What if I want to write a book?*
Hannah: *Can I use your existential crisis for a series of articles?*
June: *No.*
June: *Maybe, as long as you don't use my name.*
June: *No, don't.*
June: *You know what your problem is?*
Hannah: *I'm sorry, but you're the one having a crisis not me. I don't have a problem.*
June: *You do.*
Hannah: *Enlighten me.*
June: *You like to live through others.*
Hannah: *Huh, have you been talking to Tess or Mom?*
June: *You can use my current life but maybe you want to start fixing yours. Fall in love.*
Hannah: *Nothing wrong with me. I just like to be the observer. It's easier. Once is enough, you know.*
June: *I want to at least experience it once.*
Hannah: *You will. You deserve it. You just need to believe it.*
June: *Who are you quoting?*
Hannah: *Me, I don't copy my shit from the interviews. A lot of the quotes you read on the magazine or social media are mine, bitch.*
June: *About writing a book.*
Hannah: *Why a book?*
June: *Maybe it's the stage of my life or what I'm living. I'm not sure.*
Hannah: *A memoir? I'll send you the creative writing books I've read along with some workshops. Don't expect to finish your first novel today. It takes time.*
June: *You should be teaching me.*
Hannah: *I like you too much to agree.*
June: *What are you teaching next semester?*
Hannah: *Literature of American Cultures and Literature and Philosophy. I added an online class, Creative Prose.*
June: *Again, teach me how to write.*

Hannah: *No, I am an asshole. I like you too much to be one with you.*

June: *Liar. That's not why you have a big waitlist. Your students love you.*

Hannah: *Fine, I don't want to. Happy?*

June: *Why?*

Hannah: *You're too demanding. Any new fun anecdotes for the magazine?*

June: *You don't want to teach me how to write but you like to use my material.*

Hannah: *What can I say? Ethan and I think your life is ... hilarious.*

June: *When are you and Ethan going to get together?*

Hannah: *I love him but we're friends and he's engaged. In case you're about to throw something like, well, he's not married, stop.*

June: *Did I tell you I slept with the hot guy from Thanksgiving again?*

Hannah: *Tell me more. Still as hot.*

June: *We've been sleeping together ... and I get to touch every tight muscle of his taut body.*

Hannah: *Deep ridges?*

June: *Yep.*

Hannah: *How's the package?*

June: *He packs.*

Hannah: *Hey, I read your fucking thirty day list. Have you done anything with the list yet? I like the do something good for a stranger.*

June: *What do you suggest?*

Hannah: *Let me research the area and I'll find something for you.*

I look at the list I've been trying to update, and scratch write a book.

June: *Where are you spending the holidays?*

Hannah: *Surprisingly in California. I convinced my family to fly to me. Ten years in a row.*

June: *Go home, Hannah.*

Hannah: *Love you, June, I'm on a deadline. SS.*

June: *SS?*
Hannah: *Speak Soon.*
June: *You're an English teacher.*
Hannah: *I love language and bending it is ... delicious.*

"Funny picture or something outrageous happened?"

I look up at Sterling puzzled by his question. "What?"

"You're smiling and you said you'll be sitting down here to drink your coffee and read the news. I'm wondering what you were reading."

"I'm chatting with Hannah," I inform him. "She's one of my closest friends. I ..." I wave a hand. He doesn't need to know the story.

"The magazine owner?"

I nod. "Co-owner. She's also an English teacher and funny."

"Your appointment is in an hour. Get ready, we're leaving in thirty. Beckett is driving us."

"Can we not have your entourage following us everywhere?"

"Sorry, it's a precaution. I'll try to ditch them when we go to Steamboat."

JUNE

❄

"Am I too dressed up for the occasion?" I ask Sterling as we enter the clinic.

Suddenly the black trousers, silk blouse, and my Burberry jacket seem out of place. I should've worn something like what he's wearing. He's dressed in a pair of jeans, a black Henley shirt, and a pair of boots. According to him, it's not cold enough to wear a jacket. It's freezing but I won't argue with him. He looks sexy. Tall, lean, yet muscular and powerful. His presence relaxes me.

"There's nothing wrong with what you're wearing, you look hot," he says, holding my hand.

Not sure about hot, but I think the outfit says, look I'm ready for my next meeting. Not, let's make a baby. Of course, there's no dress code to create a baby, is there?

"June Spearman," I say. "I have an appointment with Dr. Travis."

The receptionist looks at her monitor, then at me and types fast.

"You're all checked in. The nurse will call you when she's ready for you."

I nod and take a seat.

"Do you want me to go in with you?" Sterling asks. He hasn't released my hand since we left the apartment.

"It's okay, I'll be fine."

"June Spearman," the nurse calls out.

Sterling squeezes my hand again, gives me a quick peck on the lips, and says, "I'll be here waiting for you."

As I walk away, I turn to look at him. His face doesn't say much. But I swear I feel like he wants to stop me. I wave at him. He winks at me.

"Follow me," the nurse orders and I do. Instead of heading to the examining room though, the nurse asks me to wait in the doctor's office.

The doctor comes in rather quickly. He holds a folder and when he looks at me, he frowns.

"June, we received your lab tests earlier today," he states. "We'd like to take another blood sample to verify the results."

My heart thuds hard because two months ago, when I started the hormone therapy I was doing fine. Healthy and ready to have a baby.

"Is everything okay?"

He shrugs. "It might be. This is good news for *you*. I just need to verify a few things and we might want to refer you to a different doctor. When was the date of your last period?"

Well, that's a weird question. I pull out my phone but answer, "Last week," and pause, verifying my calendar. "Yes, the twenty-sixth. But it was a light spotting. It happens sometimes. One month my period is light. The next four I'm in big pain for a week or so, feeling like I'm going to bleed out. Then, I don't have a period for a month or two."

"You had spotting in November?" he asks. I nod in response.

He scratches his head. "We definitely need that test or an ultrasound. What's the date of your previous period? The one before November twenty-fifth?"

"Twenty-sixth," I correct him and laugh when I check my calendar. "October thirty-first. I know, Happy Halloween."

I roll my eyes.

He taps the folder, looks up to the ceiling, and says, "That's almost six weeks of gestation."

Gestation? What is he talking about?

"What?" I ask, confused.

"Did you have sex between October and November?" His question worries me.

"Fucking Sterling, do I have herpes or syphilis?"

He laughs. "Oh, not at all. You're pregnant."

"What?" I shriek. "No. I can't just get pregnant? That's impossible. You said it'd take more than a miracle."

He takes his writing pad and a pen out of his pocket. "Take this to the pharmacy. The receptionist will give you an order for a sonogram. I want to make sure the gestational age is correct. I think we should start counting from October thirty-first. That's—"

"Five weeks and four days," I say, touching my belly. "This can't be happening. I chose a good candidate. We faxed you the information yesterday. This can't be happening. I made a very detailed plan."

Suddenly, I'm furious because *he* just destroyed my plans. I march to the waiting room where he's expecting me. When he sees me, he grins at me. Someone should sucker punch him just like he did to me.

"You!" I'm so fucking angry at him.

How dare he do this to me?

"I can't believe it," I say pointing an accusatory finger at him. "You ruined everything."

His eyes widen and he lifts his hands. "What did I do?"

"I can't believe it. I had a plan. We chose a candidate—together. This was foolproof. I ... what the fuck, Sterling?"

Yeah, what the fuck?

I'm ... pregnant.

Finally, I'm pregnant.

And suddenly, overwhelmed with a million emotions, I begin to cry. Fucking Sterling Ahern rises from his seat and hugs me tight. His hand rubs circles on my back and his voice is soothing.

"It's okay, whatever happened isn't the end of the world," he assures me. But he doesn't understand how my world just changed—again.

"Ms. Spearman, here's the order for the sonogram and the prenatal vitamins. Dr. Travis printed this list for you. He would like you to see an ob-gyn to begin tracking your pregnancy. Congratulations."

"You're pregnant?" Sterling asks with such joy that I cry even harder.

"Thank you," he says, taking the papers from the nurse. "Babe, you're scaring me. What happened?"

"I'm not sure. This wasn't supposed to happen. I can't have babies," I assure him. "But now, this can't be possible. And I want them, but this isn't how I planned it."

"Let's go to the car," he commands, as if trying to put me together because I just broke into a million pieces.

❄

During the drive, I'm quiet, numbed, and I can't think further. What am I supposed to do? As we park, I realize we're outside a different building. Not his house.

"Where are we?" I ask.

"Give me a second," he says and leaves the car with Beckett.

Beck walks away with a paper in his hand, while Sterling gets back in the car.

"Let's talk," he says. "What happened at the doctor's office?"

I fidget with my lower lip. This isn't supposed to be happening. "My plan was foolproof. What am I supposed to do now?"

Finally, I lift my gaze and look at him. I've never seen him look at me so serious. Maybe that's not the word because the nostril flare is anger. Why is he upset?

Because he knows, and he has rules and if this isn't part of my plan well, it's everything he's always avoided.

Pull yourself together, June. This guy is about to demand you lose the kid. Which I won't do because I've been waiting for him and he's mine—or her. Us against the world.

Taking a deep breath and wiping my face I say, "I'm pregnant. Please know I wasn't being deceptive. With my condition—"

"Stop right there," he interrupts me. "What exactly is the problem? Isn't this what you wanted?"

I shrug. "It makes everything difficult. Having a baby from an anonymous donor was easy. In the future, when I get the question, where is Dad, the answer is simple. Now..."

Taking a deep breath, I look out the window wondering how I'm going to handle this pregnancy and the baby's future.

I should just go back to San Francisco. There's no point in staying. The reason I did it was because I wanted to be near the fertility clinic while this happened. Far away from the office because I need to rest.

Now... I have to leave because I'm bad at rejections and getting attached to this guy is getting too easy. But now he's going to kick me to the curb, and it'll break my heart to see how he's going to reject the baby.

Our baby.

"Well, everything is different. I don't want my kid to feel unloved but what can I say when they ask, where is my dad?" I ask figuratively and look at my lap realizing he's holding my hands. "We won't ask you for anything. I'll have my lawyer draw a—"

"Stop," he orders. "Don't say shit that's going to piss me off, Juniper. This wasn't in your fucking calendar and I get it. It's upsetting. If you ever say that you're going to serve me with legal papers to take away my parental rights we're going to have a big problem."

"But I know how you feel about family."

He nods. "Maybe so, but I was thinking that if I love my nephew like he's mine, I imagine my own child might be the same—even more."

"You barely see your nephew."

"That implies seeing my brother and sister-in-law. I like them both but not enough to move to Tahoe."

Beck arrives at the car and he taps on the window and opens the door. "They're ready for her."

Sterling nods and looks at me. "Come on, the technician is ready to see you."

STERLING

PREGNANT, I REPEAT INSIDE MY HEAD. I'M HAVING A BABY.

This thing with June is starting to feel a lot bigger than I intended it to be. The thought of her carrying another man's baby was destroying me.

We could have a baby together. I could learn to be a father. Fuck, I want her so bad in my life that I offered to be the godfather of her child. Well, what do you know, I'm the father. But the way she saw me, the anger in her eyes and her words. I don't know where I stand.

You're not seventeen, I remind myself.

I can be whoever the fuck I want and I'm bulldozing my way into this situation if she won't allow me to do it in a friendly fashion.

"We have to make an appointment," she says, looking at Beckett.

"It's set," I announce. "I'm sure you know how things work when you are a celebrity and have money."

She presses her lips together and nods.

"Let's go and see if the doctor is right. You haven't even told me how you came to that conclusion."

Not that I doubt her, but we just had sex two weeks ago. Seeing how upset she is about this, I can see that if possible she would treat me like a male praying mantis and eat my head before the day is over.

"Why are we going through the back?" she asks.

"Part of the illusion. Important public figure," I explain and ask Beck, "Did they sign the NDA?"

He nods.

"How, he just walks in with the order from the doctor?"

"Haven't you heard the man for the past couple of days? We have procedures. He knows how to handle these situations."

She opens and closes her mouth. I can see she's not thrilled about the special treatment, nor am I but I have to use my name to speed the process. We have to talk. I have to convince her of many things including that I can be a part of this baby's life.

As promised, the room is ready. Beck stays outside and closes the door behind. The technician is already in the room.

"Good morning," she greets us.

June and I greet her.

Without missing a beat, the nurse begins to explain what to expect, "This is a transvaginal ultrasound. Take off your clothes from the waist down and use this blanket to cover you. It's similar to a pap smear. I'll be back in a couple of minutes."

June looks at me and then the door.

"Sweetheart, I've seen everything. I'm not leaving you."

She rolls her eyes and does as she was told. The technician comes back a couple of minutes later and explains what she's going to do.

"We're just confirming the gestational age. You paid for a 4d sonogram which we can't do at this point but please feel free to come back in about ..." She moves the wand inside June around and says, "There they are. The gestational sacs. They're about two millimeters each."

"This isn't possible," June says. "You can't get pregnant a week before your next period."

The technician looks at her and smiles. "Do you have regular periods?"

"No, I have PCOS but I was taking hormones to get pregnant."

"That explains the multiple birth. Your ovulation isn't regular, and you might've ovulated not only late, but released more than one egg."

She hands me over a grayish picture and says, "Congratulations, it's twins."

My heart drops to my feet because one was already mind-blowing but two.

"You can get dressed and leave through the back door. I hope to see you soon."

"Twins," June says as she gets dressed. "They run in the family but … now, what am I supposed to do?"

"Take a breath," I suggest. "Smile and enjoy the news. I thought this was going to make you happy."

She sighs and we leave the room. By then, Clark is with us. Beck thought it'd be a good idea to have more than one security detail covering us just in case anyone recognized me. We drive to the penthouse in silence. I'm not sure how to act or what to say when she's so quiet and frazzled.

When we arrive home, she climbs up the stairs and Beck looks at me. "What do you need?"

I point at the stairs. "For her to open up and let me in. Do you have any advice?"

He shakes his head. "You're on your own, man. Any other chick would be asking you for money and a ring. She's different. I like her. What do you want?"

"Them," I answer. "Not sure how it's going to work but I want June and my babies in my life. You said it, she's different."

"Let me know if you need anything."

"Bring in a new guy. We need a detail for her."

"Are you still going to Steamboat?"

I look upstairs and shake my head. "No, most likely we'll be staying in town."

And if I have anything to say about it, in this house because she's not going anywhere. Not if I can convince her to stay with me.

※

When I go upstairs, she's in my room pacing around and tapping her phone.

I lean on the doorframe and observe her. Suddenly, she stops and looks at me.

"Sorry for sounding ungrateful. It's just that this makes it harder. I can hear my brothers demanding I marry you because when it comes to me, they behave as if we're in the early nineteen hundreds and I should be a kept woman."

I can't help but laugh. She's too independent to follow the rules of old society.

"What do you want?"

She shrugs. "In regards to?"

"Your future."

She smiles and touches her flat belly. "Them. They talked about the possibilities of multiples and how the hormones might release more than one egg, but I need to rethink everything."

"Why not enjoy it?"

"I will, soon. The house should be ready next week but maybe I should go back to San Francisco. Being a single mother of one seems like a lot of work but two? I'm sure Mom is going to help, and Dad."

She smiles.

"Yeah, I have the entire family. This should be okay. Jeannette will help too." Then, as if a new plan just popped in her head, she looks at me and says, "You can be as involved as you want. I just beg you, don't hurt them. If you think this is too much—"

"Don't hurt them or you?" I ask directly and walk toward her taking her hands. We're not walking around each other without facing the big issues. "This is me telling you upfront that we're in this together. Stop pushing me and telling me that you don't need me around. Maybe you don't, but they do. It'd be nice if you don't take their choice of having me around away even before they're born. Do we understand each other?"

With wide eyes, she nods.

"It's just that you said it once, family isn't for you. Being involved makes you part of the family even if it's unconventional. We have to come up with rules."

"June, why do I feel like you're putting a wall between us?"

She looks at me and frowns. "I've no idea what you're talking about."

"Juniper, there's an unspoken rule between us. We don't bullshit each other. Be honest with me."

"I like you, Sterling," she pauses, looks at me from head to toe, and says, "a lot. Like, hmm, wouldn't it be awesome if this was real and we had more than just great sex."

Okay, so she's scared and we're two fucking frightened people who have been hurt so much they can't see how this can work. Well, we'll make this work. Fuck, this better be worth it.

"Thirty days around you sounded doable because as a fantasy it works. I know when it ends, and reality starts. I was going to pick up my things and leave with my new life. But now, you're part of my future—even if I don't want it. We need boundaries."

"Boundaries," I repeat. "So, you're switching our dynamic."

She nods. "It's best if we keep our distance."

"What if I tell you that I want this to become our reality?"

JUNE

Sterling stands so close to me. His scent is fresh, sandalwood with a tone of citrus. The man who helps me fall asleep and not think about anything but him. He helps the anxiety go away.

I'm tempted to put my arms around his neck. I wish I could ask him to quiet my mind from the noise going on. To be as happy as I am because we're having a baby.

Two babies!

Instead, I remain still.

"June, stay with me. Your mind is already running a million miles per hour," he says.

It impresses me how he knows those small details about me. I like it but I want to hate it. For some reason, he makes me just want to relax and let him take charge of us. But I can't possibly delegate such an important matter.

This isn't a Christmas fantasy anymore. It's a Christmas miracle and is so precious I need to take care of it like a crystal heart.

"You don't mean it," I answer. "You said it, no bullshit allowed. I respect your parental rights. We'll come up with an arrangement that will benefit them above everything."

He snorts. "I get it. You can't take a chance on an irresponsible, unreliable, and negligent man. What if I offer to change for them … for you?"

My heart shrinks because he doesn't see himself the way I see him.

"Why do you think you're all those things?" I frown. "You have nothing but ugly words to describe yourself sometimes and other times your ego doesn't fit in the penthouse. You're reliable and dedicated. Look what you've created for yourself. The life you've built. Your art is everywhere, and you own a business."

"It's my father's. I just help my brother."

"Don't belittle what you do," I say, upset. "Are the properties your father's too?"

He shakes his head. And if I have anything to say about it, in this house because she's not going anywhere. Not if I can convince her to stay with me.

I cup his cheek and ask, "Who hurt you, Sterling?"

"No one," he says quite forcefully. "Give me a chance to …"

"To what, Sterling? I don't think we're in a place to offer each other anything but a friendship. We barely know each other, and we just can't do whatever we want when there's a child involved."

"Two," he corrects me and grins smugly.

"Let's start from the beginning," he says with a gentle voice. "But not here. Pack your things, we're going to Steamboat."

The last thing I want is to get in a car with him. Especially when the news hasn't sunk in yet. I'm tired. No, exhausted and hungry.

"I have to go out for a little while. You got my number if you need me. Pack, take a nap." He takes me into his arms and whispers, "It's going to be okay. Don't think too hard. It's only day one. Enjoy it. Congratulations, you're going to be a mom."

He kisses the top of my head and holds me for a couple of extra minutes. What does he mean by let's start from the beginning? And how can I stay away from him when all I want is for more? As if I hadn't cried enough, the hot pressure behind my eyes builds up once again.

Sterling helps me settle into the bed and lies right beside me. I inch closer and close my eyes.

"Give me an hour, I have to tie up a few loose ends before we leave."

❄

I SLEEP FAR MORE HEAVILY than I intend because when I wake up the room is almost dark.

"Hey," Sterling says, he's inside the walk-in closet fixing his bag. "I was about to wake you up."

"What time is it?"

"Almost five," he offers. "Winter isn't my favorite season. It gets dark before dinnertime."

I try to smile and that's when I realize he's right. There's a wall between us. Before today it was easy to trust him because I had nothing to lose and now, I'm not sure about many things.

We can't just jump into some relationship. We have to win each other's trust. Just because he's seen me naked, doesn't mean we have the kind of intimacy that couples or even friends have after years of friendship.

Sterling turns on one of the lamps. The light's dim, but I can see his soft green eyes looking down at me. My stomach clenches for a second as I imagine he's going to lower himself and kiss me.

"We have to leave," he murmurs and grins. "We're not running away but we're ditching the security team."

"Why do you have them?"

"The fans can get crazy," he answers. "Let's get some of your stuff packed."

"Thank you, I ... sorry for the way I reacted."

He shakes his head, looking amused. "Sometimes, June, it's good to know that I'm so good at shit I can make the impossible happen. My ego and I are pleased with the results. We have some kind of superpower."

A grin rises to my lips. "Of course, you are pleased."

He extends a hand to help me from the bed. I hesitate for a second because what I really want is to pull him over to me. My attraction for him hasn't decreased. In fact, I think it has intensified.

"Lead the way, superhero."

※

MY PARENTS always drove us to the mountains every weekend to ski during the winter and part of spring. That's how Alex, my brother, fell in love with snowboarding and extreme sports. It's how I became his PR manager too.

Mom tried to find someone who'd represent him. His agent is okay, but he needed someone to care for his image. The person they hired was good but once I went to college and learned how to do it right. I took over his career and started signing other athletes, actors, and the rest, as they say, is history.

I just wanted someone to look after him the way Mom always wanted to. She insisted no one worked for his benefit, just for their percentage. Mom always said no one would be good enough because they always looked after number one. I did a good job even after he retired, I still make sure he's well represented.

After I sell my business, I'm taking him with me. No one touches Alex's career but me.

Mom says he's my favorite because I can boss him around. At least, he allows it. I love Jason and Jack too but they're a pain in the ass.

"I like Alex," Sterling says. We're by the deck having dinner, enjoying each other's company and just chatting. "He was good. I actually know his brothers too. Well, your brothers."

"You do?" I frown.

He nods and points to the house next door. "Have you ever come with them to Steamboat?"

I lean forward and it clicks. The house next door is Jackson's. I didn't recognize it. In my defense, it's dark and all the driveways look a lot alike. Plus, I never drive up here. It's either Jackson or Jason who are at the wheel and I'm always too busy answering emails or preparing a news release to pay attention to the road.

"So, you know them," I conclude.

"You can say that," he says casually, and I think this is more than I know them.

He's maybe a year or two older than Jackson. Jason is right behind them. I bet he partied with them. I could give him a hard time about it just because he's trying to hide it, but I won't.

"They're not going to be happy about this," I inform him.

"Tell me more about you." He brushes away what I just said.

"Have you ever had a serious relationship?" I ask because we've been talking a lot about me lately and I don't think we've covered anything about him.

"Serious? Nah, I don't go beyond a night with a woman—maybe a weekend."

"Ha, guys like you are made, not born. You remind me a little of my brothers."

"That concerns me, in what way?"

"*'I'll never be in a serious relationship, they're not for me,*' they always say," I answer. "And do you know why? Because something happened that changed your life and scarred your heart."

"You believe that?"

"Of course." I nod and go on a tangent about my brothers.

When Jason was twenty-five, he was left at the altar by a bitch who couldn't even say no when he proposed. She made him organize the wedding and then ran away. Then there's Jackson's ex-wife. The bitch used him and stole from him.

Don't get me started with Alex. He's had not one but three relationships all of which he swears weren't important, but they broke his heart. The last one, Charlotte did a number on him. She broke up with him after the car accident where the doctor said—he might not walk again. He's walking again but needless to say, his career ended that night.

At least Jason and Jackson have found love and their hearts thawed. What about Sterling?

"Fess up," I say after I finish my rant.

"You hate them," he concludes.

"They were bitches with my guys," I respond. "The point is that after what they did, my brothers became playboys but deep down, they're close to Prince Charming. Something happened to you that made you believe love isn't worth it. What was it?"

He shakes his head and leans his head back resting it on the chair while admiring the stars. If it wasn't for the fire and the blanket covering us, I'd be inside reading a book. But he made this so comfortable I want to stay here. Such a shame I can't enjoy it out here with a a glass of wine.

"Kara," he says. "She was my best friend while growing up and dating her just happened. I thought we wanted the same things. During senior year of high school, she came to me saying, 'I'm pregnant.'"

He laughs. "Then, she said she wouldn't keep it."

"Why not?"

"She couldn't have my kid. I was irresponsible, unreliable, and if it wasn't for my parents' money, I'd have nothing. That once we graduated, we were over. We wanted different things. I researched what I could do. She couldn't just give the kid up for adoption without my permission. So, I tried to talk to my parents. They had the resources and money to get custody of the kid. They said that I was too irresponsible to keep a fish alive."

"Did you kill a fish?"

He rolls his eyes. "I was six."

"What happened to the baby?"

"It was a false alarm, she wasn't pregnant but needless to say, we broke up after that and that was it between us."

"Your parents?"

"Never thought much of me. They died hoping I'd mature and become them."

I nod, well that explains a lot. Does he love himself? I lean my head on his shoulder. "I trust you with our babies and I'm sure you won't become your parents."

Giving him a shy smile, I add, "But we can become mine. They're awesome."

We fall into a comfortable silence. It's just us and the night until he asks, "Who was your first love?"

"Even though I'm a serial monogamist, I don't think I've ever fallen in love."

"First boyfriend?"

"Dan, I was almost sixteen. It was during the summer. He was cute, and we always did things together. I remember him fondly. His family moved to Seattle after junior year."

"First loves are different from the love of your life," he says. "I loved Kara; she wasn't the love of my life."

I whistle as I sigh. "Well, then how do you know?"

"When it happens, it'll catch you off guard. Change your entire life. It'll be a soul deep connection and you'll need each other like you need air to breathe. Maybe when you find love the stars shine brighter and everything that used to be dull has a new light. She'll be your favorite feeling, even when you can't understand it. The best place you've ever been in and the one you want to stay in forever."

"Sounds like you're talking from experience," I say, my heart squeezing, not sure if it's envy or something else.

Not that I'm jealous of the woman who captivated his heart.

"Still figuring things out," he mumbles and kisses the top of my head. "We should start buying baby books. I don't want to suck at being a dad."

I close my eyes, resting my hands on my belly and for the first time today, I just enjoy the moment and forget about the future. Tomorrow everything will look different.

JUNE

Last night I fell asleep in Sterling's arms and he brought me to the main bedroom but didn't stay with me. It felt empty and different from the previous days. Is it wrong to miss him when I'm asleep?

After his definition of falling in love, I think he stole a piece of my heart. A big chunk more likely. I refuse to complicate things between us, and I need to pull away from him. Not sure how or when I'm going to do it.

Sterling suggests we spend the week enjoying the news, the fresh powder, each other, and relaxing. Next week we'll discuss our future. After breakfast, he suggests we go skiing. I accept, and before driving to the slopes, we stop at my brother's house to *borrow* my equipment.

The perks of being close by to Jackson's place are many. Let's hope he doesn't catch me because I don't have the energy to explain to him why I was at his garage—and spending time with his neighbor.

During our second round going down the mountain, I have a bad feeling. That gut-clenching feeling when you know shit's about to hit the fan and you're doomed. It's hard to concentrate, but I try my best going behind Sterling who isn't happy about it. As I explained, I'm better at following than leading.

This entire day has been weird. I feel as if someone has been watching us since we arrived. I know when Sterling notices the guys because he speeds up and I follow right behind.

My stomach tightens and my legs wobble, but I don't let them give up. We're going to speed up and make it to safety. After that, Sterling better have a good explanation. Unless he has bodyguards because someone wants to kill him.

I swallow thickly.

The fear runs through my blood along with the adrenaline. When we arrive at the bottom, I pull off my helmet and visor and glare at him.

Before I can say a word, there's a loud bark behind me. "You're working from home? This isn't home."

When I turn around, I realize the guys who followed us were his bodyguards. Great, we have company. What happened to we'll be alone for the next week?

"I'm at home. This is a free country," Sterling says upset. "You can't be just following us everywhere. I have a life—I want it back. She doesn't deserve to be caged too."

"We have a protocol," Beckett says and turns to look at me. "You are the one who is making him break all the rules. You should know better."

"Oh my gosh, is that Sterling?" someone somewhere all of a sudden screams.

"Yes, it's him!"

In less than five seconds women and men are screaming nonsense.

"Ahern, sign my boobs!"

"Code four," Beckett says.

Suddenly there is a bunch of women sprouting like daisies in the middle of spring. One of them asks for his babies and the one next to her is crying hysterically. I've seen this before when I was doing PR for a boy band, but this guy is not that famous. Is he?

Okay, he's famous, hot, and who wouldn't want to have his babies?

One of them says, "I told you he was the guy in the restaurant. I knew these would pay off." Then she glares at me and mouths, *Bitch, you can't have him.*

Whoa, what is happening?

"Kiss Steamboat goodbye," Beckett says, grinding his teeth.

"Fine, I need you. Please get us out of this one," Sterling finally speaks. Looking at me, he takes a deep breath and continues, "I don't want anyone to touch June. Make sure you put a detail on her and no one takes her picture. We're not leaving Steamboat yet though. We'll manage … get whoever you need to cover us."

"Oh, fucking hell." Beckett starts giving orders around.

The next thing I know we're in a black SUV. We drive it for a couple of miles until we reach another unmarked, white truck. After four car changes, we're finally at the house, disoriented.

"What the fuck is going on?" I ask upset and ready to puke.

Beck looks at me, then at Sterling and asks, "She doesn't know. Does she?"

Sterling shakes his head.

"What do I have to know?"

"For a public relations person, you seem a little clueless," Beckett declares and I'm pretty offended. "Our boy here has a flock of followers everywhere he goes. Some of them believe he lives for them. They're the kind who stalk houses, boil rabbits, and pretend to be knocked up so they can get a proposal."

"The dangerous kind," I conclude and shiver because I've dealt with this kind with Alex and some of my other clients.

Everyone thinks stalkers only affect actors. They don't. Alex had one living in his house when he was out of town, she pretended to be his wife. She spent a couple of years in an institution after her lawyer pleaded insanity.

"Bingo, she is as smart as she looks. Maybe you can explain to this guy why you two need us around at all times because clearly he still thinks he's a free man to roam around whenever he wants."

My chest squeezes and I understand why he is so isolated. My heart hurts because he's the kind of guy that likes to be around people even when he doesn't look like it. I grab his hand and squeeze it.

"It's fine," I say reassuringly. "If we have to go to another secret mountain to ski, we can do it. Unless, you want just to stay in the house and watch movies or draw. We can always keep our equipment on, it's not like they'll recognize you."

He smiles and links our fingers together. "Whatever you want to do," he offers. "We can go back to the city. It's safer. I don't want to put you or the babies in danger."

"Are you sure you want to stay?" Beck asks.

"How did you find us?"

"You were walking around town freely. There're several pictures of you and fans wondering if you're here. Hashtag sterlingwatch is trending. I got the call. If we're going to do this, I think you should move into the Viking Lane house."

"Do you want to go home?" Sterling asks.

I shake my head. "These guys will be around if we need to go out, they can join. Now, I understand the apartment downstairs."

"Sorry for what happened back there. I let myself believe this could be different," he apologizes, putting his arm around my shoulder and pulling me to him. "I'd never let them touch you."

"I'm okay," I assure him. Then to change the subject and break the tension I ask, "Do you know when the furniture for Viking Lane will arrive?"

Beckett sighs and looks at Sterling. "I had to speed things up. It arrived earlier today. Even if you don't want to move there, we increased the security. HIB securities added cameras and a new keypad."

"So how does it look?" I try to redirect the conversation. "I need to order some Christmas decorations."

Beckett shows me pictures of the house. The furniture looks great. It's just like how I imagined it as I picked each piece. I just need to order the bedding for my room.

"Too pink," Sterling protests.

"It's my place," I argue. "Pink couches."

"It doesn't matter, we have to compromise."

"That's only the office. *My office.* The rest of the house is gray, white, and black," I explain as I show him all the pictures. "The master bedroom is going to be pink because of the bedding, but I'll take it with me."

He looks at me suspiciously and says, "Fine, you have good taste. Get neutral bedding, I'm not sleeping on a pink bed."

You're not sleeping with me, I don't say.

"We just need a Christmas tree," I add, wondering if I should buy an artificial one or a pine.

Scanning the house where we're at, I find the perfect spot and walk toward it. "Here."

"What's happening there?" Sterling's frown deepens.

"That's where we're setting the Christmas tree," I answer, already thinking about the colors that will fit the house. "What do you have in storage? Any red or gold ornaments? I mean, if you already have a color scheme, I'll work with it, but shades of red and gold would pop with your decor."

Sterling looks at me. More like he gives me a nasty glare. "We don't do Christmas or celebrate any holidays. The only colors I have in this house are in my studios and well, you. Their only purpose is to create art."

I frown and place my hands on my hips. "I'm a color?"

He grins and winks at me. "A very special one but let's not digress."

"What are you saying? I'm not allowed to have a Christmas tree and fill my space with cheer and joy."

"You can do it for the rental. That's your place for the next year and you can set Santa's Workshop in there if you want to."

"Hmm."

"You're judging me."

"Not at all. Just wondering how we can get the pine here and we'll need decorations," I continue and turn to look at Beckett. "You seem like a resourceful man. Can you make this happen for us?"

Beckett smirks. "Red and gold?"

"Add some silver too it if you can find it. And if you see some decorations that'll go with the ornaments, send me pictures before you buy them. The place looks bare."

"No," Sterling protests.

"I'll have the team work on it. We'll help you trim once we have what you need, Miss Spearman."

"Thank you, Beck."

"Juniper, I swear," Sterling utters, his face is red, and it's kind of funny to see him flustered.

"Yeah, you can swear. I've heard you for the past week. Also, I know you can use some holiday cheer and I'm here to share it with you."

"Over my dead body." He sounds stern.

"Beck might be able to do that too if you insist," I say. "He seems to be trained to take down bad guys and I bet he knows how to hide your body and make your disappearance look like a holiday miracle."

He doesn't say a word, but I see there's a smile playing on his lips.

JUNE

❄

"We're only staying here for a few days," Sterling says after we're done decorating the house.

It took us three days to make it look like a home. Or as Sterling likes to call it Santa's Workshop. Beck had to send a couple of guys to Denver to pick up the stuff I had ordered online. There wasn't much around town to decorate.

Sterling protested, but he helped us—against his will, he repeated that several times. I don't believe him. The man had an opinion on where things should go and would look appealing because the reds weren't homogenous. His excuse was my continuous puking. Morning sickness has caught up to me and it's not pretty.

Earlier today, I said we needed a painting that matches the current décor, like a cabin in the middle of the snowed mountains. He pulled out an easel and paints from his studio and began to work on it.

I'm fascinated by him. It's like watching Bob Ross's show, except this guy is taller, hot, and he's not telling me to paint happy trees everywhere.

"How long have you been doing this?"

"When did I start painting? Around the age of one, Mom gave me crayons so I'd shut up and stay occupied while she was busy raising her other children."

"You sound bitter about your siblings."

He shrugs. "I'm not. Honest to goodness, I'm glad she fostered them, and they had a place where they could live safely. In fact, I'm still in touch with a few of them."

"I can hear a but in between the lines."

"According to Mom I was lucky to have been born an Ahern. I had everything. Everything except my parents' attention. For some reason, they could manage caring for five or six foster kids at a time but when Sterling needed anything, they sent me with the nanny."

Sterling is right, I'm glad they could care for those children but how about their son? "That's awful."

He shrugs. "If I acted like my foster siblings to get attention, they didn't care. At some point it was just the craft room, my crayons, and me. They were my outlet. Sports were okay, but I always had to finish the day drawing or doing something with my hands."

"How about the fans?"

"I blame social media," he states. "At the beginning, it was a tool to sell and show what I could do but suddenly it got out of hand. My followers believe they know me and own me. It's been bad. So bad that when my mother died, I couldn't attend her funeral."

Walking to where he stands, I grab his palette and the brush and set them on the table next to the easel. I reach up to give him a hug. I try for it to be friendly. But when my body meets his, the spark between us lights up. His arms go around me, and my heartbeat spikes. In an instant, arousal fills the space between every thump.

"Sorry," I say, and release him fast.

The wave of nausea claws at my throat. I try to force the food down while running to the bathroom. My stomach contracts violently and thankfully I make it to the toilet.

"Baby, it's okay. I'm here with you," he says smoothly, the baritone of his voice soothing me just like his big hand drawing circles on my back. "Beck's searching for crackers."

The low rumble of his voice is comforting.

"This isn't going to be pretty," I say, once I'm done.

Brushing my teeth, I spot him leaning against the doorframe looking at me. Smiling.

"Sorry."

He shakes his head. "I'd rather help you with this than have that conversation while you pity me."

"I didn't." I shake my head. "I wish you wouldn't have to go through this or while you have to face it you weren't alone. Alex wasn't. He had us—me. Where's your family?"

"As I explained, Wes lives in Tahoe, I try to avoid them because Abby and Lance don't deserve to be in the middle of this shit show. I'd die if anything happens to them."

"If you ever need a friend."

"You don't need my shit either." He lifts his arms and holds his head tight, shaking it. "How are we supposed to protect the little ones? Maybe you should..."

"Hey, I get to decide if I want to deal with your shit or not. I can manage crazy well enough." I reach out for his hand. "You have a team. I know people too and we will protect our babies. They'll grow happy and safe."

He pulls me to him, and it's become like a habit for us to end up entangled. His mouth kisses the top of my head. "What if they do something to you guys, how am I supposed to live with that?"

"You don't look like the kind of guy who'd be afraid of anything," I mumble. His face is so close to me.

"Not usually, but you scare the fuck out of me, Juniper. I don't understand you and yet, you're so easy to read. I trust you. I stopped trusting people years ago."

"How about your brother?"

"He's different. We get each other and the same with Abby though I have to keep them away…"

"Safe," I finish his sentence, and he nods. One of his hands slides to the back of my head, his fingers lacing through my hair. Gripping gently, he tilts my head. Our gazes connect and those fiery eyes are burning—for me.

Sterling's mouth brushes slowly over mine before settling in. The tenderness of this kiss is unsettling, arousing. My knees give out, thankfully he's holding me so securely with one arm. One of his hands comes up to my jaw. Our tongues swirl around. The kiss is endless. Soft, loving. New to us.

His hand slides down my hips, pushing me closer to him. He's unbelievably hard—everywhere. We kiss and I feel a desperate ache. I'm losing myself and my thoughts. This isn't taking things slow or starting from the beginning, it's—

"Juniper Spearman, what the fuck are you doing here?" I hear Jackson's voice and there's a loud banging on the door. "June, open up. I know you're there, open the fucking door."

"Who is that?" Sterling asks, gasping for breaths.

"June, I can't stop him for too long." I hear Alex's voice. "Open up, Junie bee."

I grunt. "My brothers," I say, untangling myself from him. "Are you ready?"

JUNE

Ever since we were kids, Jack has always known when I borrow his things without permission. I knew going into his garage might trigger some camera. He has a tight security system. To top it all, I stole his Internet connection.

But hey, I needed *my* equipment and a faster Internet connection. Sterling's slows down when we stream movies.

What's the best way to keep myself connected while we are lounging?

I hooked up my electronics to his Internet.

It's Jackson's fault. The guy always brags about *it* being so powerful he can connect to it even if he's hiking a couple of miles away from his property. Well, the geek is right. I'm less than a mile away from his home and I've been taking advantage of it.

He's in the city, after all. He won't notice until he comes back and hopefully by then, I'll be gone.

"I thought you had bodyguards to take care of unwanted company," I growl, marching toward the door.

He snorts. "I'm sure they know and that's why they're letting your brothers do whatever they want—to interrupt me."

We walk to the main door and what do we find?

Not one, but three very annoying Spearman brothers glaring at me—and Sterling.

"Juniper?" Jackson crosses his arms.

"Jackson?" I cross mine too and give him the glare. He might be taller, older, and meaner but I'm not letting him treat me like I'm five years old. "Do I go to your house and bang on the door at odd hours of the day? Mom will be disappointed with your manners."

"This isn't your house," he corrects me. "And it's three o'clock."

Sterling surprises me when he says with a firm voice. "It is her house."

We all turn to look at him. I'm totally dumbfounded by his answer.

"I like you, Spearman, but watch your tone." He looks at my brother darkly.

"I thought we were friends, man," Alex says with disappointment. "You're breaking the bro-code."

"Seriously, June," Jason says with a tone of disappointment and brushes some strands of my hair. "At least fake it."

I open my mouth to protest but stop myself. Saying I look like shit because I've been puking all day is going to open the can of worms I want to keep closed for a few more weeks—months even. Maybe I'll have the babies and tell them about it when they turn four or eighteen.

"Not to interrupt this amusing family reunion, but it's cold as fuck outside and she's not wearing a jacket," Sterling says, pulling me into his arms. "How can I help you, gentlemen?"

"Let's go home, June," Jackson orders.

Sterling turns to me, his eyes soft. "Do you want to leave?"

I shake my head.

"You heard the lady. She's with me," Sterling barks back. "She's also not your property to order around."

Butterflies fluttering and all aside, I compose myself. Because no one wants to speak with a puddle of mush, and say, "I came with him and will leave with him."

"Mom doesn't know where you are," Jackson starts nagging. "She's freaking out because she went to visit you and your neighbor said you're out of town. The first thing she did was call me because I'm responsible for you when our parents are out of town."

"Jason." I appeal to the one who isn't as possessive.

"You know I love you and I support you," he says. "But this wasn't cool. At least text me your whereabouts. What's going on with you? I heard you're selling your company."

"You took the month off," Alex adds. "What if I need you?"

"This is so unlike you," Jackson says frustrated. "I get it from Jeannette but you ..."

"Me what, Jackson? Just because I decided to change my life that doesn't mean I'm a failure. You changed yours, just like Jason did. I can't search for my own happiness?"

He frowns and closes his mouth tight.

"Cool it," Jason says, and I realize he's talking to Sterling who is glaring at Jackson, nostrils flaring. "Let these two fix their shit."

"We're moving this party inside. It's getting cold, baby," Sterling whispers. "Gentlemen, you're welcome to follow us or leave. As I said, it's cold and she doesn't have her coat."

My brothers frown and surprisingly, they follow us.

"Look, I'm not sure what's happening with you," Jackson says. "If I'm upset it's because you upped and left without telling us. If you want to sell your company, that's cool. I'll help you find the best buyer or with whatever you need. Why didn't you come to me and ask for help? You used to tell me everything and call me every day. Now I'm lucky if you answer my calls once in a while."

"It's Em, I already told you that," Alex answers for me. "She hates your wife."

"I like her," I mumble.

Okay, confession time. I hated her when they started dating but it's because she lied to him. She wasn't upfront with him—later I found out that he wasn't either though. I did what I had to do. My brother married an ugly bitch once, I wasn't going to let that happen again.

Now, I like her. In fact, I like her so much that I won't tell Jackson she's the one who helped me realize I needed a break from the family. To step out of my comfort zone and reach for my dreams.

The last thing I want is for them to end up having problems because of me. Though, he's right about me pulling away from him. Emmeline brought it up too and as I promised, I'll fix my shit with him once I am done with myself.

"Sorry, it's been a hard couple of years," I conclude. "You have your life and I didn't want to…"

"You have to come to me, June. We're in this together. The five of us. I have Em and the girls but that doesn't mean the four of you aren't important."

"Same goes for me," Jason says. "What's happening? You don't like Eileen? I can dump her if you want."

I laugh. "You're an idiot," I tell him, knowing he loves Eileen too much to even consider leaving her for an overnight trip.

Knowing him, she's next door waiting for him.

"The point of this isn't that we're the five musketeers. It's why the fuck are you with *him*?" Alex protests.

"That's enough, Alexander," I protest.

"He's just like your clients. Selfish, self-absorbed, and not what you need," Alex concludes.

"It's like you're looking in a mirror," I retort. "Me being here isn't any of your damn business. I'm spending a few days with Sterling Ahern in Steamboat."

"We're heading back to the city early next week," Sterling informs them. "We'll be happy to send you the address of our home in Denver, and I appreciate it if you're discreet about it."

"Your fans, man. If something happens to her," Alex says with a warning glare that matches Jason and Jackson's.

Sterling nods and hugs me tightly. "My security team has orders to keep her safe. She has her own security detail."

He has a bodyguard assigned to me. Two new guys arrived after the incident on the slopes. I already set a few alerts to make sure there aren't any pictures of us together. So far, no one has spotted me.

As for how long I'm staying here is to be determined. We're having a good time together. No, it's great. But also, I know I have to figure out our future. Being with him isn't sustainable in the long run. He's not the kind of man I want to raise my kids with. Not because he isn't a great guy but let's get real. The groupies, the chaos, and the lack of human interaction aren't good for children.

I wouldn't take away his parental rights. However, I don't see how this co-parenting would work. I'm giving myself some time to just relax and not worry about a future with Sterling in my life. He lives here and I live in California. That's already a problem.

So, for now I'm not going to think about any of this. Once he goes to his penthouse and I ... I should just go back to San Francisco.

"Hey, we agreed, no thinking," Sterling whispers in my ear and kisses my temple. "Gentlemen, if you don't mind visiting hours are over."

Jackson glares at him. He hates him. This is going to be messier than I thought but if I got over Em, he can see past whatever is bugging him about Sterling.

"Dinner," Jackson says.

"What about it?" I ask.

"Both of you are invited to have dinner at the house. Em wants to see you," Jackson explains.

I look up at Sterling who shrugs. "It's up to you."

"Okay," I agree.

"See you in a couple of hours then," Jackson says, and my brothers leave.

"Intense," Sterling says. "I've always said that guy needs to get that stick taken out of his ass."

He glances at me amused. "We should play with yours."

"Leave my ass alone." I slap him playfully on the chest. "We're not having sex, Sterling."

"We just had a moment—interrupted by those three." He takes me into his arms and I'm a sucker for his embrace, so I let him hold me.

"But we shouldn't." My voice comes out throaty because his mouth is so close to my ear it makes me shiver and needy.

"I want this, and I know you do too." His mouth drags gently along my throat. "There're so many things we haven't tried yet. So much I need to learn from you. What makes you tremble, cry my name with pleasure, and smile."

"Can we learn to be friends?" I change the subject, because, God, I want all that. "Think about the little ones, not us."

Sterling presses my hips closer to his. The heat between us intensifies and I can feel how hard he is—for me. He winks and I dissolve into a puddle of wanton goo. I'm unraveling and he hasn't even touched me. I close my eyes and hold back the whimper. "Us, I keep thinking about the four of us. But in the meantime, I want to replay how we made them."

"We shouldn't," I insist. "Let's learn how to get along and be friends. This isn't a marathon. What's going to happen if we ruin it before they turn eighteen?"

He nuzzles into the sensitive place behind my ear. "You're the only one ruining the moment. Live by it. Let things go."

"Let me get ready for dinner," I say, pushing him away before I succumb to his seductive voice and tender touch.

"We have a couple of hours."

I wave a hand around my body. "I look like I've been puking all day."

He studies me. "You're not telling them?"

"Are you bringing your security team to protect you?" I lift my hands and pretend to wash them. "Because I won't defend you."

He laughs. "I can take them if you want to tell them."

I shake my head. "Mom should learn about it first, then Jeannette," I sigh because I'm not sure what I'm going to tell my parents just yet. "Actually, let me call Mom. She might drag Dad to Denver and cancel her trip to ... I can't remember where they were going after Peru."

When I reach my phone, I grin and before I dial Mom, I text Em. She'll take care of Jack.

June: *What is wrong with your husband?*

Em: *Sorry, tried to stop him.*

June: *It's okay, I handled him. Heads up would've been nice.*

Em: *Sorry, I meant to text you but I'm dealing with the girls and ... Multitasking after motherhood gets complicated.*

June: *No hard feelings. I'm calling Mom.*

Em: *Good, she's worried. I haven't told her anything, but she knows I know what's wrong with you.*

June: *You're a good friend, love you.*

Em: *I'll give Jack a little hell. Love you too.*

"That's a scary grin, what did you do?" Sterling asks.

"Payback," I say, winking at him while I call Mom.

JACK

"You have no right," Em, my wife, chides me. "As I said, call her, confirm she's there, and invite her over."

"I controlled myself," I say defensively. "She's in Sterling Ahern's house. We've seen the crazy parties he throws. What if she's having an orgy?"

"I've been at those parties," Jason adds. "We used to party together. Do you think I want my little sister with him?"

Eileen stares at him and crosses her arms. "What are you saying, that I should dump your ass because when you were younger you were …"

"But I'm not like that anymore," Jason protests.

"How do you know he is?" Em questions and stares at the two of us. "I saw the parties, but they stopped long ago. The only guests he has are Wes and Abby. You know, I'm happy she's with someone different from the usual assholes she dates."

I glare at Em because she knows something. She's hiding something from me.

"How long have they been together?"

She smiles and shakes her head. "I don't know. You just told me they are together. I haven't even confirmed it."

I run a hand through my hair. "What's happening to June?"

She shrugs. "That's her story, not mine. You know my rules."

I'm not sure if I should be pissed at them or glad that they're finally getting along. It was killing me that my sister kept her distance from me, and Alex continuously said it was Em. I love them both, I can't leave my wife but losing my sister hurt.

"Is she safe?"

"You have to trust her. She's not a kid and you're not responsible for her. Barging into your neighbor's house trying to drag her home was pretty fucked up. If she's not mad at you, I am. June isn't going to show up at your door and say, I got married."

"Jeannette moved to Hawaii—after doing just what you said," I complain.

"We have tickets for January. We'll be there for a couple of weeks. Now, help me cook. The girls are taking a nap."

I nod, put a hand behind her head, and take her mouth. She's right, I shouldn't have acted the way I did. I could blame my mother for calling me at five o'clock in the morning mortified because her daughter wasn't home. Why didn't she call me last night? She didn't want to wake up my daughters. Better call me at five when she can wake up the entire house.

"Love you," I mumble. "Not sure why you put up with me."

She smiles and hugs me tight. "Because you love me as much as I do you. We just have to work on a few kinks because you're going to be a better father than you are a big brother. If you ever do that to our girls, I won't be happy."

"I'll try." I don't make promises I know I'll break.

Now the question is, how am I going to ensure that June doesn't end up with that fucker?

STERLING

"Invite them to stay with us," I say, while June's on the phone with her mom.

"I'd rather talk about it in person, Mom," she insists. "No, I didn't get married like Jeannette, and Teagan wasn't a stranger."

June rolls her eyes and then smiles. "Yes, Mom, *that* Sterling Ahern. I guess you're right, he's cute. We met around Thanksgiving. Uh-huh, that guy. Well, I guess you're right."

She nods and then her face turns a pale green and by now I know what's happening. I take the phone and wave at her. Slowly, I follow her to the bathroom.

"Junie," her mom calls her loudly.

"She's currently busy. Where do you want me to send the jet to pick you up?"

"Who is this?"

"Sterling Ahern, ma'am."

"Hmm, I guess we have to settle a few things before we fly to Denver. Will you be eloping if I don't get there on time?"

I chuckle. "I can promise I won't marry her until I get your blessing, ma'am."

"Call me Ariadne or Aria."

"You have my word, Mrs. Aria," I say. "When do you want the plane?"

"We can buy our own tickets, but it's very kind of you to offer."

"I insist."

"Well, let me talk it over with James and I'll let Junie know. Please, take care of her. It's nice to know that she's letting someone take care of her for a change."

"I will, it'll be a pleasure to meet you."

"Sterling, darling, do me a favor, tell her to eat fresh ginger. That should settle the nausea."

"I…"

"Be good to her," she says and hangs up the phone.

Somewhere in this house is my common sense. I can't find it. I could've misplaced it when I first saw June. Which if that's the case, it means I lost it weeks ago. If I trace my steps for the past few days, I could figure out exactly what happened. Other than, I lost my ever-fucking mind.

But how could I not when June is so fucking fantastic and refreshing?

She's witty, smart, and doesn't let me get away with shit. Also, she's beautiful. Those lips, like a ripe forbidden apple. Tempting. I can't get enough of them, of her. I can stare at her for hours, trace her body with my hands and mouth. Draw her. I have so many mock-ups of her. Her image is ingrained on me. If I wasn't busy touching her, I'd be molding her with clay.

What do I do? Invite her parents to stay with us. Offer the jet to pick them up and I spoke with her mom on the phone. When was the last time I met the parents of the woman I was hooking up with?

Never. I knew Kara's because they lived next door.

Why am I being nice? Well, first of all, this isn't hooking up anymore. It's a relationship that June refuses to acknowledge and I'm trying to establish.

Again, my common sense is either not working or ... I freeze when I see her coming out of the bathroom. She's literally glowing and looking fucking beautiful.

"What did Mom say?"

"Call me Ariadne or Aria," I answer.

She narrows her gaze and twists her lips. "Did she scare you?"

I sigh. "Her words were, 'Tell her to eat fresh ginger. That should settlethe nausea.'"

Her eyes open wide. "How does she know?"

I shrug. "She sounds scary. Like one of those women who knows everything."

"Mom is that scary," she confirms. "Is she coming?"

"Yes, but she doesn't have a date. She'll let us know after she discusses *it* with James. I assume that's your dad. Should I be worried?"

I rub my face because it's been years since I worried about what others think about me. But I care about what her parents will think of me and if they'll accept me. These are the people she admires and loves the most. If I want to be in her life as more than the father of her children, I have to impress them.

She shakes her head. "I'm going to take a shower. Is there any way that you can find me fresh ginger?"

"On it." I wink at her and she slips from my reach before I can grab her and kiss her.

She owes me.

Ahern: *We need fresh ginger.*

Beck: *Already got it along with ginger tea. They're in the kitchen.*

Ahern: *How did you know?*

Beck: *EMT training. You're whipped.*

Ahern: *You should've warned me about the brothers.*

Beck: *Where's the fun in that?*

Ahern: *We're going to Jackson's house for dinner. Bring a guy with you, make them believe you know how to do your fucking job.*

Beck: *I know how to do my fucking job. But I'll put up a good show just because I didn't like how they talked to June. She's feisty, I like her.*

❄

"Beck is amazing," June says as we settle in the den to watch movies. "He deserves a raise."

I agree. At least, a bonus. It was pretty badass of him to arrive at Jackson's house before us and scout the perimeter to make sure that it was safe for June to arrive. He claimed that June required a different protocol than me.

He even did a full body scan on Jackson to make sure he wasn't armed.

"Thank you for coming with me," she says as she settles in the couch.

"That was … intense," I say, because, wow, I have partied with Jason and Alex, but June and Jackson are exhausting together. "So, there's like a rule about not letting you and Jackson play Pictionary, Monopoly, charades, and what else did they say?"

I think I get the dynamic between them. Jackson is the oldest and he rules them all. Except the little one doesn't agree with it and she challenges him. June is six or seven inches shorter, four or five years younger than her brother but she questions every move and decision he makes.

She admires him though, and I think Jackson is proud of his little sister but doesn't let it show. Today, I learned they aren't allowed to play some games because they go from fun to war.

I said, let's play charades. Emmeline, Jackson's wife, didn't know about it either and she seconded my suggestion. Alex said, we can't. Jason thought, they're older and more mature and thought it would be okay.

Jason then gave us the list of games they stopped playing when they were teenagers.

"It was a stupid game," she complains.

A stupid game she lost three times. She can't act for shit. Pictionary was fun until she began criticizing Jackson's drawings and he did the same.

"So, you dated Cole Radcliff?"

Her brothers brought him up during dinner. Alex is the one who mentioned him. Cole Radcliff played professional rugby for a couple of years. Then, he became a model and is now an actor. He's not good but women would watch him because of his shirtless Instagram presence.

That's the problem with social media, we can reach more people than a sitcom or a movie. We're more approachable and once we get a solid follow, we lose our private lives. We also get a lot of companies asking us to be the face of their products. I earned a lot of money that way while my father was alive. I didn't need the money, but he hated seeing my face sponsoring products —I was a sellout.

I regret my youth so much, mostly the part where I worked hard to become famous to annoy the fuck out of my parents. I did a great job and also showed Dad I could make more money than he could give me. Of course, I lost my freedom while I was at it.

She shrugs. "Not my finest moment. He seemed like a smart person and I ... I don't know what I was thinking, okay."

One moment she's upset and the next she's laughing. "He married only a few weeks after he said, 'Sorry, June, it's not you, it's me.'"

"You're fucking kidding me?"

"Nope. That's what happens all the time. They break up with me and the next person they date happens to be the one."

I don't have words, who wouldn't want to be with a woman like her? She's smart, funny, strong, beautiful, and understanding. Not the kind of woman I hook up with because she's the dangerous kind too.

The one who thinks for herself and knows what she wants.

She's going to rule the life of whoever falls in love with her ... and why do I want to be *him*?

I look at her flat belly and wonder about her little miracles. Ours. The thought of having children never occurred to me. This whole ordeal confuses me. I'm conflicted by my past and the present. The only future I allow myself to live and my fucking head hurts because today was one of the best days of my life. And every day I've spent with June is memorable.

Traveling around the world, learning new techniques to improve my craft, meeting people who impart their knowledge is fulfilling and yet, nothing is as ... I can't even find a word to describe what I feel when I'm around her.

I should know better than keep her around. I am who I am, and I'll never change. For her though ...

"They're leaving tomorrow for Denver," I finally speak. "Should we leave?"

She frowns and laughs. "You're scared of my brothers, aren't you?"

I'm scared of you, of what I can do to you. That maybe the way I want her now might be just temporary and, in a few days, I'll be done with her and I'd hate to hurt her.

What if I hate our babies? What if they hate me?

I should stay away ... but it hurts to even think that I won't meet them.

What's the alternative though?

"Nah, it's just that you have a list and so far, I don't think you have checked off many of those."

She scratches her head and goes for her iPad and clicks it. "I ordered the crochet kit. If we make a list of all the sex positions we've tried, I'm sure I have accomplished at least twenty new things. Not sure if I can get a tattoo. That's a big commitment, and I'd rather do it after the babies are born."

"There're a few things we can try tonight if you want to," I offer, trying to change my mood.

Words can be hurtful, and some actions can define a person's life. I don't want to say that my parents and Kara defined me, but they did a great job fucking with my mind. It took me years to understand that their opinions doesn't matter but this situation with June is making me second-guess my life and what I believe is best for me.

"You know what you need to do?" she suddenly asks.

I arch an eyebrow, take her hand, and pull her with me toward the room. "Order a spreader bar?"

"No, I've been thinking about your fan problem. Close your social media accounts," she says out of the blue and firmly.

"Just like that? Poof," I say, pretending to wave my hands like a magician.

She nods.

"What about my art? That's how I sell it."

"You don't," she growls. "Do you have any idea how many hoops we have to jump through to get your pieces when one of our clients *need* them." She draws quotes.

I laugh and shake my head. "What do you need? It's yours," I offer.

"You have a gallery. If they want your pieces they can go there," she says.

"I use it for other artists, not me. I stopped selling my art in there," I explain. "Anita, my assistant, manages it."

"Then open a second one for *Ahern's masterpieces* in New York, Rome, Paris. You don't have to be there. Make sure you hire the right people to manage it. Emmeline can get the right people. She knows everyone."

"What would happen when I close my accounts?"

"They'll know your life is no longer open to them. Maybe keep your Twitter. You use that as a forum to advocate for causes you believe in."

"Did you google me or study me?"

She shrugs. "I just don't think it's fair that you live so isolated. There has to be a way to give you some of what you lost back."

"Leave well enough alone, June," I request because I don't want her to get more involved than she already is.

More involved than carrying your babies, a voice says inside me.

"If you ever want to fix it, you know where to find me," she says, and I listen to what she says between the lines.

Our paths are coming to an end. And yet, I wonder why we crossed them.

STERLING

❄

June and I fall into a comfortable routine. We have breakfast then ski during the early hours to avoid crowds and fans. When we're back, she takes a nap and thankfully the ginger has worked for her. The morning sickness is only happening during the morning. Tomorrow we're heading back to Denver.

Her parents arrive in a couple of days and we want to be settled into the house before it happens. I'm going to miss this. Denver is going to be back to reality and facing the facts. What are we going to do with our future?

Once her family learns that she's expecting they're going to hate me and convince her that I'm not the best person to raise a child with—let alone two.

After we cook dinner together, we come to the den to watch a show or a movie. I'm usually with my sketchbook in one hand and a pencil in the other one.

"What are you drawing?" she asks from the couch.

"You," I answer.

"Seriously, what are you drawing?" she insists.

I cross my heart. "I'm dead serious. You seem to be the only thing I can think of when I touch a sketchbook and when I'm with you, I just want to capture your essence."

She smiles but I can tell she doesn't believe me. The guys she's dated in the past felt threatened by her and tried to destroy her self-esteem. No wonder she believed the only way to have a child is by a mail-in order of sperm.

Well, I thank fuck it was me who fathered her children. Though, that has me tied into knots. This isn't what I wanted—ever. Why would I want to bring a child into this world? An Ahern for that matter.

But I know they'll be more than Ahern. They'll have June in them and she's a strong woman. They'll be just like her. All this should be freaking me out. It's not. My only concern is how I'll convince June to stay with me because *we belong together.*

It's like she's completely mine.

The possession is incomprehensible. I don't care about owning anything. Why do I have the need to claim her, protect her?

When we sleep together, I pull her into my embrace before we fall asleep. She doesn't want to have sex, so we don't confuse each other, but so far, she hasn't kicked me out of bed. Thank fuck, I don't think I can sleep without her.

God, I'm not sure what I'll do if I can't change and if I can't convince her that I'm good for her. Stay away, send enough money to make sure she can support the children. The kids deserve a good father. That's not me. Some kids grow up just fine with one parent. What did Kara say? You couldn't even keep a bug alive, Sterling Ahern.

"Are you okay?"

"What?"

"Are you okay?" June repeats. "You look … distraught. Is it because my parents are visiting? It's okay, you can stay away."

I smile. "Nah, it's … nothing."

She leaves her computer on the coffee table, closes it, and walks to me moving the sketchbook from my hands. She smirks when she sees what I'm drawing.

"Seriously, my chest?"

"It's beautiful."

"Flat," she argues.

"Your boobs are perky, round, and magnificent."

"B cups aren't attractive."

"They are for *me*. I can fit them in my mouth and suck them while I fuck you."

She places my sketchbook on top of her laptop and sits on my lap. "What's going on?"

"Nothing, gorgeous girl," I say and brush her soft locks away from her face.

I'm salivating for her. I want to undress her and touch her body. Skirting my hands under her sweater, I find her beautiful breasts. And I pray she lets me touch her. My dick is getting hard. Her mouth on me would be just perfect, she gives the best blow jobs in the world.

She places her hands on the sides of my face and gives me a soft peck. "Don't distract me with sex. We're not having any of that. Something just happened. Your face changed. In case you didn't know, you wear your emotions. Any change and I know."

Don't leave me.

As I mentioned, the fucking common sense is gone. I am about to say something stupid. People think I have no discipline but hear me out, I have more than anyone in the world.

Two years of self-imposed celibacy. Seventeen years controlling my feelings and keeping my heart away from anyone—including this woman. Though she's fucking breaking my determination. I can fuck any woman I want without feeling more than an orgasm.

With her …

"What are you doing to me, June?"

She shakes her head. "Not sure what you're talking about, but I wish you'd open up to me. I trust you, why don't you trust me?"

"You've gotten more out of me than a lot of people have in years, please don't ask me for more."

Because dammit I'd give it to her, and it'll be hell to recover after she's gone.

"June, I respect your rules and boundaries, but, baby, I'm a hot-blooded man and if you keep wiggling yourself on top of my dick, I'm going to fuck you."

She leans closer and kisses me gently. "I'm not sure what to do with us, Ahern. Thank you for being patient with me."

"Anything for you," I say and don't let her go. I'd rather sport a pair of blue balls than lose her. I love having her body nestled between my arms. "Always."

STERLING

❄

Every artist struggles to find their inspiration. Seriously, ask anyone and they'll confirm that there's a time in our lives where we seem to have a block. Creativity comes with lots of flaws while we try to find perfection.

In fact, we artists are flaws searching for the best part of us. I had that happen to me during my late twenties when I was living in France. Nothing seemed to work. Every piece I tried to create ended up in the trash.

It's funny how things work because my landlord at the time picked up every piece of trash and sold it as an Ahern original. He made a lot of money and retired. That wise man taught me to enjoy what I had instead of looking for what I didn't.

It's crazy how our nature as humans is to search for what we call happiness. Which is an abstract term. What makes one happy doesn't make the other happy. A great example is the holidays. There're so many people who are miserable during this season because they don't have what others do.

It'd be so different if we search for the real meaning of the season. If we found the magic of what's important again. Money isn't everything. Look at my parents, they were loaded. My father worked himself to the ground. He actually died of a heart attack while at work. He promised the world to Mom and never delivered.

Once Dad died, she tried to give herself what he didn't. Unfortunately, her life was cut short too. They worked hard to find happiness and I don't think they ever found it.

This is where my problem lies.

I've been living a fulfilled life. Everything I do brings me joy. I'm content. Happiness isn't something on my radar. My legacy is my art. Five hundred years from now, I hope people recognize me as they do Auguste Rodin, Praxiteles, Donatello, Giacometti, and so many others.

It's a big reach, but I want to be that famous. I am in fact as famous as them, but not sure if my fame will continue after I die or if it'll die with me.

At least, that was my goal up until a couple of weeks ago.

As we leave the house in Steamboat behind, I don't give two shits about my legacy. My worry and the root of my block lies next to me, in the passenger seat.

June fell asleep a few minutes after I pulled out of the driveway. She's tired since we spent most of the morning skiing. I'm glad she's asleep because I can't deal with questions about my childhood and I don't want to learn more about her.

Not when I'm afraid this might be it.

All night long, I kept thinking about how I'm going to convince her to stay with me at the penthouse. Let's send her parents to the house. I don't want anyone near what I'm trying to build for us. I can't find the words or a good excuse. It shouldn't be a problem, except, I can't explain why I don't want this to end.

I have sixteen days left with June. Two without her family hovering around her. The babies give me the perfect excuse to be close to her, but not with her. If I can't pull this miracle off, what's left? Phone calls every other day to make sure she's okay. Video calls to see the babies and at least for eighteen years, I'll have many excuses to go and see her wherever she lives.

I want fucking more. Birthdays, Christmases, first steps, first words, and more than two babies. But can I?

Well, so much for expiration dates and never getting involved in my life.

My phone rings, I look at the dashboard. It's Abby. I click ignore so she doesn't wake up June, but it rings again, and this time June hears it. She stretches and yawns. Her eyes find me, and I glance quickly just to wink at her.

"You should answer," she suggests.

"It's Abby," I say as if it explains it but the phone rings again and this time, June reaches for the dashboard and answers.

"Slugger, why are you ignoring me?"

"Oh, fuck, you didn't just call me that, Abigail," I protest.

June chuckles.

"What do you need?"

"We're in town," she offers. "Come over and have dinner with us."

"I'm in Steamboat," I excuse myself.

"We should be back in a few hours," June corrects me. "We can definitely be there by six."

Abby clears her throat. "Interesting, you have company?"

"Oh, no," June says. "I'm just a friend."

"Look, Abs, we're not sure about the traffic and June might not be up to visiting anyone tonight. We had a long week and spent the past couple of days with her family. Mind if we visit you tomorrow?"

Abby stays quiet for a few breaths then she says, "Call me tomorrow to see what works best for you two. I am looking forward to meeting you, June."

I finish the call before either one can say more. Any other day I could've used an excuse to get out of seeing Abby, but I think this is just perfect. An excuse to hang out in the same house for at least another day.

When we arrive in the city June says, "I hate wintertime. It's not even five and the sun is down for the day. Can we see the house tomorrow?"

I nod, take her hand, and kiss it. "Do you want the guys to pick up takeout or should we try to cook?"

"What are you in the mood for?"

"Only hungry for you, baby. You'll have to be in charge of dinner."

She grabs my phone and starts tapping it. "Done, we're having Mexican food from a place Em loves. They should be delivering it when we arrive."

"You didn't ask Beck?"

"Nope, you're not the only person with people," she says, winking at me. "Now drive because after we're done eating, I want dessert."

My dick gets hard. It better be me. Swollen cock, tight balls. The pressure is killing me.

Fuck, will I ever be able to touch her again?

"What's for dessert?" I ask hopeful. Maybe it's her pussy and I can eat it for an appetizer.

"Just ordered flan and churros," she says. "I'm eating for three, after all."

"Sounds delicious," I tell her, happy that she's coming to the penthouse with me.

How do I convince her to stay with me forever?

※

"You had a girl in your car yesterday," Abby says as she enters my studio.

"Give me my keys back," I order.

She wiggles them and shakes her head and starts roaming through the studio looking at my work. Then, stops at the table and scrunches her nose. "Please tell me I'm not looking at your girlfriend, naked."

"Stay away from my studio," I grunt.

"She's pretty." Abby ignores me. "I didn't have to see her tattoo."

"Actually, she doesn't have a tattoo. It's on her list and—" I stop myself. "Never mind. What do you need?"

"How long have we known each other?"

"Decades, what do you want?" I ask annoyed because fuck her and her need to know everything that's happening in my life and fix what's not broken.

She paces a couple of times and then stops in front of me.

"You let me talk to her and we're having dinner tonight."

I shake my head. "No, I haven't agreed to that."

"June did."

"How?" I ask and cross my arms.

"Beck gave me her phone number." She grins knowing she has the upper hand. "Two weeks, huh."

My bodyguard is a dead man and June better have a good reason to be talking to Abigail. Being polite doesn't count.

"Get it over with, Abby. Circling around shit isn't your style. What do you need me to tell you so you can be on your way?"

"She sounds smart. Nothing like the girls you've been with," she explains. "Not that I ever got to talk to them. Still. This one is different. I can feel it. So, I want to know how I can help because I don't want you to—"

"Fuck it up?" I ask and try not to glare at her. "Not to worry about it, it's nothing serious. You know me, Abs. I'm a loner."

She shakes her head. "Seriously, who fucked you up?"

Abby has been asking that question for years. She swears I'm a catch but since someone broke me, I just can't see more than a quick fuck and the next rush of adrenaline.

"So, we're going to your house tonight?" I change the subject.

"No, actually June invited us to *the house*."

Her words feel like a slap in the face because, *fuck,* she moved out without even telling me. I knew she was going to leave because neither one of us has an excuse to stay together but *still.*

It stings.

"Abby, leave," I say.

"Sterling," she sighs. I ignore her.

Instead of working with clay, I go to the changing room and get ready to work with metal. I can't deal with anything else. I have to destroy.

Abigail remains standing in the same place. Her face saddened as usual. She's pitying me.

"I won't see you tonight, will I?" she says.

"Goodbye, Abs."

I storm to my workshop in the next room, slamming the door shut.

❄

I SWALLOW the anger and put the hammer down as my arms shake of exhaustion. I close my eyes trying to get ahold of my emotions. I've been doing this for hours and the tightening feeling continues clogging my throat. My anger comes like an impossible build up of steam, burning on the way out.

Why did Abby's visit leave me this angry?

Because June left the penthouse. That's it. That's my breaking point.

She left me.

When I open my eyes, I realize it's not anger. It's sadness. It's a hollowness that holds shards of glass between my soul and body. That's pain. Pain of losing June.

Fuck, have I made a mistake?

When it comes to my future, I always thought I was in charge and I had everything figured out. It's not. Thinking I had everything I needed was the biggest lie of all. Until now, I was empty.

It's fucking scary when you realize there's something missing in your life.

I finally recognize that my life is a sham. Art is my trade but not what completes me. I'm lonely. I don't live in the moment. I hide behind my creations. There's an empty space in my heart. And what a fucking twist of fate when I realize that the only thing I need to fulfill my life is my family—the one June and I are creating.

JUNE

❄

WHAT WAS I THINKING?

The problem is, I haven't been thinking much—if at all. I've been playing make believe with a guy who lives in a different reality. Since we had dinner with my brothers, it seemed logical at the time to invite his family to spend some time with us.

Now I have a table set up for five people, dinner in the oven, and a text from a woman named Abby apologizing that an emergency arose, and her family won't be showing. What she didn't say is that *the family* included Sterling.

I knew this would be over when we came back to Denver. But after this morning I was hoping it'd be different. It's ten o'clock at night and he never showed up. I turn to look at the tree I trimmed earlier and the house that now looks like a home. Why did I go crazy decorating the house? It looks as if Santa set up a subsidiary of the North Pole. I had hoped he'd stay with me at least for the remaining of my stay in Colorado.

Not gonna happen. Let's erase every idea I concocted in the past few days. Having my parents over for Christmas is going to fill the void. I hoped Sterling would get to know Jeannette and my parents, they're important to me. But this is for the best.

If this is it, he should at least send me a text, give me a call, or something.

My fingers play with the phone. I've been writing texts to Sterling and erasing them before I get the nerve to hit send. There's nothing to say, is there?

Message received. He didn't want to move the party to a bigger place. It's over. Time for reality, plans, and a future where we don't exist as ... nothing. We aren't a couple.

Who are you kidding, June? You were never anything.

Still, I'm afraid there's always going to be some small emptiness in my heart that will never go away. He'll be around, hopefully. We have to sit down and define our future—if he wants to be a part of it.

Having a baby is my dream. I've been ready for this moment. His decision won't affect me directly. I should call my lawyer tomorrow to have him draw up the paperwork. On second thought, I should email him now.

Once I set everything in motion, I start cleaning the kitchen. Setting the leftovers in my new containers. The ones I planned on using for the next couple of weeks to send Sterling with food. Though, I also found the perfect room for him to set up a studio. Actually, it's the pool house. How crazy was I to think that maybe he could set up something and ... I sigh and continue working when I hear the door open and a big thud sound.

"You couldn't fucking call me?" Sterling yells. "Is there something wrong with your phone?"

I frown at him, crossing my arms. "Who do you think you're talking to?"

"Why did you leave a note when you knew I wouldn't read it until I came home?"

I frown and hold my breath. His face is red, his eyes on fire. He's wearing a T-shirt and a pair of unkempt jeans. His hair is tousled and if I know him well, I can say he just came from the studio.

"Hi to you too," I say, immune to his temper.

He waves the paper I left taped on the fridge and sets it on the countertop. "Let's move the party to the house. Seriously? What am I supposed to do with that, Juniper?"

I shrug because I'm too tired to understand what he's doing in the house or fighting with me.

"What does this mean?" he asks. "What party are you talking about? For a woman who is so methodical, this doesn't make any sense."

I was too busy trying to make today perfect. Another great example of how my behavior is affected by him.

"I was busy, it made sense to scribble the note," I begin my explanation, but it doesn't make much sense, so I expand. "Your sister-in-law called my phone to invite us for dinner. I suggested they join us. I had to decorate since my parents arrive tomorrow and I want to be ready. Also, the penthouse isn't child friendly. By the way, she agreed with me. At the time it seemed like a good idea to just pack my things and move in here. Maybe you'd join me. Earlier it—"

"You want me here?" he interrupts me.

I nod, having trouble speaking, not because I'm afraid of this version of him. It's because I'm trying to understand what's happening. Are we fighting? Why is he upset? I'm confused as to what we're discussing, even when it seems pretty clear.

He marches to where I am, his body pressing mine against the counter and his arms caging me. "Why didn't you call me?"

"When I'm working, I hate to be interrupted. You don't like interruptions either. I've watched you. You said you'd come for lunch, but your sister-in-law called at nine and I had to leave to get everything ready."

He closes his eyes and slumps his shoulders.

"I can't anymore," he says, leaning his forehead on top of mine.

The hot drift of his breath, his mouth so close to mine. I'm desperate for a kiss. My heart thunders inside my chest. My body weakens and I don't understand what he can't do until it hits me.

Stay with us. Don't leave me.

Instead, I say, "It's okay."

At least I emailed my lawyer. He answered back, explaining me my options. In a few days, he'll send the documents for Sterling to sign. It's his choice. Visitations, custody, rescinding his parental right. Tomorrow, Mom is going to insist I go home where she can help me.

There's a strange pang of pain in my heart. It's not love, I insist. We just met, but perhaps, I gave up a lot more of myself than I wanted to. "Really, I get it."

"No, you don't," he argues. "You've no fucking idea of what's happening to me."

He's right, because even with the anger in his eyes he kisses me tenderly, molding my body against his. His warm and sturdy arms secure me firmly. My hands search for an anchor, his neck. I link them behind his head losing myself in the kiss.

The things he does with his mouth, his tongue, how he deepens the kiss hungrily and so urgently. It's as if the world is about to end and this is the last second we have left. He's taking his last meal, his last breath, and his last beat.

Perhaps he's trying to give me one last kiss before we part ways. Our story won't have an ordinary happy ending. So, it'll never be about the ending but the loving and how happy our kids will be after all the loving we did during our chapter.

One last time, I think and turn off my mind, letting him take whatever he needs tonight. To give me everything I need from him. He finally unravels me, and I let chaos invade me.

"June," he says, breathing hard. "I need you."

I understand him because I need him just as much.

There's this pull I've been fighting since we found out about the babies that's getting stronger every day. I don't understand it, but it's hard fighting it.

Even if I try to stop him, I can't anymore. Not tonight.

I have to feel close to him.

Let him make me feel alive one last time.

He's so different than any other man and I know that if I stay any longer, he'll destroy me. But if I pull away right now, my skin will wither without his touch. It's been craving his skin just as much.

"Sterling," I whisper before his mouth finds mine again.

Somewhere between the hot, hungry kisses, we begin to pull at each other's clothes. The need sharpens. No goodbye has ever felt this right, this incredible. Just as explosive as our first encounter and I'm afraid that nothing will ever feel as intense as this moment. As him.

So, I decide to beg him. "Take me to *our* bed, please."

The first and only time we will share it as an us.

"Please," I ask again and kiss him with lust pulsing through me.

He lifts me; I hug his waist with my legs. He takes several long strides toward the staircase and then up the stairs. We make it to the room in record time.

"Tell me if you want to stop," he says when he lowers me over the bed. "I know your boundaries and your rules and the last thing—"

"I understand," I say, pulling him down to me. "I want this, us, right now."

Nothing is real or has been real since we met. For some crazy reason since I met this guy, I let him touch a part of myself that no one is allowed to see. I allow myself to be greedy and enjoy what he offers me.

He sucks on my nipples, his tongue circling around them with the same expertise as when he kissed me. One then the other. Tugging the tips of my tits while his skillful fingers tease along my thighs, parting them. He runs them all the way to my apex. My body tightens as his thumb caresses my slit.

"I love foreplay as much as you, but tonight, don't make me wait," I order. "I need you inside."

His weight slides over me, his legs spread mine wider. My thoughts implode as I feel the pressure of him working slowly right outside my entrance.

"My sweet, June," he says and enters me, sliding his thick length inch by inch. Hot, sweet, maddening sensations playing inside my body.

A loud moan stirs in my throat.

He places his hand on my hip, pulling me higher. Every thrust is a full-bodied embrace. The raw sensation between us, the sound of his heartbeat, and his kiss is consuming me. We feed off each other's lust, moving frantically. The ache I felt for the past few hours weighing down my heart finally dissolves when the waves of pleasure make my body jerk and tremble.

What's going to happen tomorrow?

STERLING

❄

I PULL JUNE'S SLEEPY BODY CLOSER TO ME AND KISS THE TOP OF HER head.

What can I do to convince her to be mine?

In the big scheme of things, I am in charge of my life. Nothing is set in stone. Why is it that I'm not bending my own rules? I rebelled against my parents and anyone who tried to come between me and what I wanted. For the past twenty years, I've fought for what I believe is my future, for what I love, and I showed everyone that I'm capable of succeeding on my own. I've been making my mark through the world but today I realized that none of that matters.

They're insignificant compared to June and our little ones.

I used to live under the illusion that I lived for me. This is a first. The day I come to realize that there's more to what I've done in the past thirty-seven years. I used to control my emotions and June Spearman appeared into my life and proved me wrong—or showed me what's right. The woman who lives to control everything around her, taught me to release my heart and let it feel.

Looking at her, I smile. This is what I want. Having June

between my arms every night. She is who I want, who I need. The life we can forge together. Ever since Kara, I told myself the same lie again and again, that I don't deserve love and I can't love. I closed myself up to the possibilities.

Earlier, I tried to keep the lie alive but the thought of not seeing June or my children stopped me. I found the courage to fight for her. I could sit on my ass and claim that love isn't for me. It'd be so much easier to give up before anything serious starts.

Who am I kidding? We've been trying to fool ourselves. The attraction began the moment I spotted her.

If I have to ask when was the moment we reached the point of no return...that'd be our first kiss. I recall the intensity, the heat, and how I started to fall. I'm still falling. This thing we share is fragile. Forged by lust, in the middle of a wildfire. I don't dare to give it a name because it's too early.

She releases a throaty moan while still sleeping. I smile and brush away some strands of hair from her face. I then caress her flat belly, wondering how things will be when the babies arrive. They'll flip my life upside down.

Just like June.

She was unexpected, and yet, in weeks she changed everything. I'm yet to explain what exactly it is about her that made me fall for her. Maybe it's the way she cares for me.

June makes me see myself in a different way. She cares for me in a way no one has ever cared. Fuck, how I wish it was love. Maybe it is and like me, she's fighting it. Either way, I'll try to win her over.

I can't lose her.

My soul would die. I feel her sunshine fill my lungs each time we kiss. She's more than air. She's all I need to survive.

Am I ready to love her?

This feeling is so much different from what I've experienced.

I've never felt the magic I feel when I'm with June. She's a gift.

June snuggles closer to me, molding her body perfectly with

me. We're imperfect, filled with flaws but she has everything I'm missing. She completes me. What is it that I have to do to prove to her that I'm not leaving?

"I love you," I whisper before I close my eyes. Maybe soon, I'll have the courage to say it out loud.

JUNE

I'M NOT SURPRISED WHEN I WAKE UP AND FIND MYSELF ALONE IN bed. The only witness to the best night of my life. It's unlike any other night. I couldn't call it sex. It was a delirious dance of tangled bodies, burning fires, and surrendering hearts.

My heart still throbs and all the emotions we let out continue flowing through my blood. What am I supposed to do with what I feel? What is he going to do? He can deny it, but I saw it in his eyes, the burning fire but also the affection.

Sterling Ahern cares about me, just not enough to stay.

Touching my belly, I send a prayer that these two are enough for him to let himself believe he's capable of so much more than a birthday card.

The rest of this mess is on me. I'll have to fix everything that broke, including my heart. Why did I let myself get tangled in his arms and his magical make believe?

It was a moment of weakness. I let the chaos take me over and gave him all—maybe even my heart. I don't regret it. Not for a moment.

Now, it's time to go back to the old June, the one who color codes every hour of the day. It was fun to color outside the lines. Order is what I know best.

"It's going to be okay," I say out loud.

I have some nice memories from Sterling, plenty of pictures to share from the short time we were together.

"He cares for you two," I assure the babies. "He's a loving person, I know, if only he believed so himself."

Since Mom will be here later today and already knows I'm pregnant, I call Jeannette. Keeping her in the dark for this long has been killing me. It's time to search for my other half.

"Hey," Jeannette answers immediately. "Finally, are you going to tell me what's going on with you?"

"Well, you're a little feisty today," I say defensively. "What is wrong with you?"

"Hmm, well, you're selling your company, Jackson found you at the neighbor's house—with an I-just-fucked face, you have a security detail, and I'm yet to learn what you've been hiding from me for the past year or so."

"Nothing."

"June, I've let it go long enough but I'm starting to feel left out."

"I was puking, not fucking," I clarify. "Though, I let them believe that because it was better than saying something like, I was puking my brains because I'm pregnant."

"You're what?"

"I'm pregnant," I repeat. "Remember the guy I slept with during Thanksgiving week…"

Pacing around the large master bedroom, I tell her everything from beginning to end. She doesn't interrupt me.

"Congratulations on the babies," she says dryly.

"But?"

"You confided in other people and not me. I'm your sister. Not only that, your twin. Are you still upset because I didn't tell you about the wedding?"

"I wouldn't use the word upset, more like pissed and still not over it. I'm your fucking sister. Your twin," I claim, my voice getting loud. "We promised to be each other's maids of honor and you eloped. But that's not why I didn't tell you. You were too busy, and I didn't want to suck you into my drama."

"Teagan and I didn't want a traditional wedding," she says apologetically. "Sorry about it. I was caught up in the moment and … it happens you know. From everyone, I thought you'd get it. You're still my other half, but Teagan is my better half."

I'm jealous because she found love. Someone came into her life and she wasn't even looking. This is why I gave up and, of course, now I have feelings for someone. *Sterling.*

"Come and live with us," she offers.

"Thank you, but I have to work something out with *him*," I sigh.

"But you said it's over," she says, pushing the knife deeper into my heart.

"Oh, but that's between us. Not that we ever started anything," I clarify. "Sterling wants to be a part of their lives. Also, after selling the company I have to make sure I invest the money wisely. I can't just jump on a plane to Hawaii where it's beautiful but so expensive."

"In other words, you need to organize the next nineteen years of your life," she concludes. "I'm here for anything, you know that?"

"Are you coming for the holidays?"

"Shit, let me talk to Teag. It's supposed to be her family's turn, but I might be able to work something out," she says.

"I might forgive you for not inviting me to your wedding," I say, and laugh because I know that won't work. "I'm joking. It's fine if you can't be here."

Jack and Jason always spend the holidays with us because their wives don't have anywhere to go. It's horrible that Emmeline and Eileen don't get along with their families, but it's good because my brothers don't have to split the holidays.

Teagan loves her family, so she and Jeannette plan on splitting the holidays. Not being with Jeannette every holiday is going to be hard, but we'll learn to cope.

My stomach growls and I decide to head to the kitchen, and that's where I spot him. He's shirtless. I stare at the swells of hard muscles along his back. It makes me want to trace the lines along his bare back with my mouth.

I suck in a breath because I realize there're things I still want to do, and the desire hasn't waned yet. My mouth craves his hard length. I want to wrap my lips around his cock. Capture his wandering hands and slide them down to my center.

How I wish we could continue exploring each other. He's touched me in places I never thought I wanted to be touched and I only want him to be there.

Jeannette grounds me back into reality when she asks, "So now that things are over with the hot guy, are you planning on dating?"

Dating? Why is she asking that? I have children and … I stare at him.

"I'm not sure," I mumble.

"But he left you hanging just a few hours ago," she reminds me and I realize she's taunting me.

"That's what I thought," I reply.

"Hey," he says, turning around and giving me that cocky grin that takes my breath away. "I was going to bring you breakfast in bed."

"So, he's there," Jeannette says.

"Mm-hmm," I answer.

"Call me later," she requests. "I'll be there soon, okay?"

"You don't have to, but think about the holidays, okay," I whisper as Sterling marches to me.

"You need me, hang in there," she finishes the call.

Sterling smiles wider as I approach him hesitantly.

"You look tired," he murmurs. "I should've let you sleep."

Sterling touches my face with one hand, and his thumb strokes my lip, I let out a low moan.

"You're here," I manage to say.

He eases me into a hug, molding me to his body. His arms secure me close to him. "Where else would I be?"

"I thought last night was goodbye."

"And here I thought we had finally come to an agreement." He rubs my back, it's nowhere erotic like last night, more like soothing and tender. Either way is delicious. His hands are magical, so perfect. I don't want him to stop touching me. Ever.

"The question is, where do you want me to be, June?"

With me, I think, and those two words surprise me and yet make sense.

But I refuse to say anything because I don't know where I stand, and I refuse to give him more. I rest my head on his chest, the *thump-thump* of his heartbeat relaxes me. My hands go around his waist and I close my eyes.

It's on the tip of my tongue to ask him to stay—forever—because last night was delicious and seeing him always makes me smile. That's better than confessing how I'm having trouble breathing because I know we came to an impasse and there's no way to move from it.

"Those wheels are turning. I can hear them," he says. "Should we eat before you begin scheduling the next thirty years of our lives?"

Not sure what startles me more, 'we' or 'thirty.' What irritates me is him calling me out on how I schedule my life.

I stiffen and push myself away from him. "Are you patronizing me?"

Placing my hands on my waist I tell him off. "In case you haven't heard, I'm going to be a new mother in a few months. Children need a routine. I do too. If I'm lucky they'll wait until next August, but sometimes twins are born weeks before their due date. It'd be irresponsible of me to wait until they are here.

"So what if I'm trying to get my act together? There's so much to do," I say. "At least for the first couple of years, I want to stay with them. I need to choose the right buyer for my company and set the money aside so I can live comfortably for those two years."

He shoves his hands in his pockets and stares at me attentively. I take that as a 'continue with your plan' kind of gesture. Maybe it's not, perhaps he's thinking, *fuck there she goes planning the rest of her life. I'll pretend to listen and leave once she's done with her sermon.*

"Not sure how you see this situation. We ... I mean, I have to start thinking long-term about what I'm going to do. This is permanent. I was ready-ish to have one kid, two is a totally different game."

He exhales and sighs. "Where am I in those plans?"

"Where do you want to be?" I ask.

He laughs. "I just asked you that, June. Where the fuck do *you* want me?"

"It's not up to me," I answer. "I won't force you to do anything. You're the one who decides."

"Last night I thought I was clear. Maybe we have to start with some ground rules. If you need me to stop, let me know."

"Ground rules?" I ask. "You hate rules."

He rolls his eyes. "That's right, woman, you're rubbing off on me. Rule number one." He shows me his index finger. "If you need to speak to me, you call me—no exceptions. Since day one I stop doing whatever I am doing whenever I see your phone number." He smirks. "You had me since you said, *I want your property.*"

"I'm pretty sure I didn't say that," I argue.

"Rule number two," he says, ignoring me. "When you make plans, you make me a part of them, no exceptions. I'm part of this family. If you have questions for me, just ask. Don't assume. I came downstairs to prepare breakfast, I never left. I'm too old to play games, June. I want to be with you."

"How would I know that?"

"Well, it's time to settle things between us, sweetheart."

His statement is bold, I'm not sure what to expect, until he's taking me back into his arms. One hand curls around my neck, his long fingers grasping me gently. His lips find mine, his tongue demanding entrance into my mouth. I mold against his hard muscles, craving more.

He slides one hand to my ass, urging me against his hard length.

"Wait," I say as I get lost in him. "We can't do this."

"Kiss?"

"You know that your kisses lead up to a lot more, Ahern," I say between shallow breaths.

"Baby, this is just a taste. We'll get to the best part later." He bends and takes my mouth again.

This time, there's a deliberate grinding of bodies. The rhythm is fast.

"Sterling, I need answers, I can't continue not knowing anymore."

He stops.

"What do you want to know, Juniper Spearman?" he asks, exhaling loudly and holding me close to him; his chin resting on top of my shoulder. "If you want me to name the strong emotions I feel for you, I can't yet. I'm still trying to solve the mystery of what's happening inside me. You can live wherever you want, here, California … as long as you let me, I'll follow you. I don't need an address, I need you."

I move away slightly just so I can see him because this isn't making much sense.

"Look," he says, his intense gaze penetrating mine, "I know this thing between us is new, fragile, and somewhat complicated. There's an unexplained force pulling us together. I've only spent a few breathless moments with you, and I want more. A lifetime of them.

"Juniper Spearman, the only issue we have is that you don't trust me. I understand. We just met, and I haven't impressed you. My public record is shit and the way I talk about life sometimes sounds as if I don't give a fuck about my future. I do.

"Planning isn't my thing. My life is fucking chaos and some days I like to lose myself in my work. Since you came into my life, I spend my days working and thinking of you. What you need to know is that at the end of the day I belong to you. I don't know how or when you claimed me but I'm yours and I pray to the higher power that you keep me and someday we can be more. I'm not asking you for much right now, just for you to give me a chance."

"Sterling—"

He places his index finger on my lips. "No, I don't want you to say anything. Let me prove myself to you. As for your finances, *we* have plenty of money to live comfortably for several lifetimes. This house is yours. But if you want *us* to move to San Francisco or Sacramento to be closer to your parents, we will."

I look at him anxiously, wondering what just happened. My mind is trying to process everything he just said while my heart is beating at a billion miles per hour and threatening to jump out of my chest to join his heart.

Let me prove myself to you.

What do I tell him?

He didn't propose, yet; he said he wants to be by my side.

"This wasn't what I expected from you," I say once he moves his fingers away from my mouth. "It'd be easier if you leave and we set some kind of schedule where you visit the kids and I—"

"And you don't have to be wondering if I'll hurt you?"

I nod because why lie to him when I'm aware that's one of my biggest fears.

With his index finger, he crosses his heart. "Never," he promises. "I'll hurt myself before I hurt you, June. Yesterday I was pissed because I thought you left me. That's when I realized I need you more than my next breath. Again, don't ask me to define this. I'm not ready. Rule number three, don't push me away because you're scared. Rule number four, at night I can demand anything from you."

"Ha, in your dreams," I say, tossing my head back and laughing at his ridiculous rule. "I thought you weren't going to ask for anything."

"For now, no, once you agree to be mine, I'll be the neediest bastard in the entire universe." His lids become heavy and his voice huskier. "I like sex, but with you it's not just grinding bodies. Our love making is different. Your kisses linger on my lips, my body. My skin can't forget your touch—and I need you more than words can say."

I freeze as the flame in his eyes captivates my gaze. The promise between those words releases a wave of pleasure vibrating deep into the pit of my stomach. My heart clenches and so does my pussy.

"I want to make you mine every night for as long as you allow me."

Breathlessly I ask, "Is that a warning or a promise?"

"It's both, June." He gives me a quick peck. "You like when I challenge you and I like you that way."

Feeling dazed, elated, and turned on I suck on my lip to keep myself from asking for a taste of what's going to happen. But really, what is he going to demand from me?

STERLING

"What is it that you want from me, June?" I ask, making my way to the kitchen and leaving a few yards of separation between us.

Every cell of my body shrills in protest. The hunger for her increases and it doesn't matter how many times we fuck, I want more. She's a sweet addiction I never want to give up—ever.

June stares at me. "Why did you move away?"

"I don't think we can talk without a buffer between us. Unless, you want me to fuck you before we continue."

She looks at me and then paces a couple of times. "Fine, talk. I'm getting mixed signals and I'm more confused about what's happening between us."

"Just to be clear, yesterday was one clusterfuck because we didn't communicate. I was working hard to convince you to stay by my side and the next thing I know, you moved to the house." I scratch my head and ask, "You should've told Beck or someone what was happening. They believed they had helped you moved out."

"I did move out," she confirms. "I was hoping you'd move in with me though."

Shoving my hands back in my pockets to keep them from trying to reach out to her, I continue. "Well, that's what phones are for. You call me and say, hey, your crazy family is invited for dinner and I think it's time to move into the house—together."

"My parents are arriving today," she argues. "What were we going to do with them?"

I shrug, trying not to smile.

"Sterling?"

"We have a guest room at the penthouse," I remind her.

"Why would we do that? This place is bigger."

"It's my domain. This house is different. I'm trying to woo you and convince you that I can change."

She smiles and shakes her head. "I don't need you to change, Sterling Ahern."

"But I want to be the guy you deserve."

She presses her lips together and sighs. "Maybe I do need you to change a little. How about you start by looking at yourself and realizing you're an amazing guy? Yeah, your reputation is terrible but the guy I'm getting to know is nothing like *him*."

"Does that mean you're giving me a chance?"

June looks at me and I start pacing around waiting for her to let me down or to finally say, let's just go with the flow. Instead, she confuses the fuck out of me. "To be clear, I like you. I think you're handsome, smart, and good in bed."

"Ouch, just good?" I glare at her. "Can I just get something out of the way before you bruise my ego even more?"

She rolls her eyes. "How can I bruise it? It's so big and—"

"I thought we were talking about my ego, not my cock," I say playfully. "But if you bruise it, I'll let you kiss it better."

"As I was saying," she continues, ignoring my smug grin. "You're great but you're not an ordinary guy. Yet, you're different from other famous people. I'm confused. All I want is to be with a guy I can be sure of and will settle with me. I can give you a chance but is this a, let's have fun together until I'm bored or ... I mean, you just said you're *mine*."

I nod.

"That's a huge commitment but yet, it doesn't sound like you committed to anything."

"Do you want me to commit?"

She shakes her head. "Not if you don't want to."

I scratch my head. What the fuck does she want from me?

"This is going to sound contradictory, but here it goes. I don't want you to be with me because I am having your babies. I want you to be with me because of me." She frowns and then says, "Actually, if you propose because my father and my brothers start pressuring you, it's over between us. This has to happen because it feels right—for both of us. Not because we're exuding desire and want to fuck like bunnies."

I laugh. "You're cute," I say. "Adorable. If you weren't too far, I'd bend you over—"

June whips her head, points her finger, and glares at me. "Say it and it'll never happen, Ahern. My point is, we haven't been on a date. We're practically living together but do we know each other?"

"It seems like you're finding excuses to avoid what I told you. As I said, I don't need an answer, I need you to be aware of the situation." I place my palms flat on the island and lean over, closer to her. Our eyes meet and as I hold her gaze, I repeat, "I. Belong. To. You. I'll take whatever you give me. No, I'm not proposing. Even if your father points a gun at me."

I've never felt more vulnerable in my entire life. Not even when I was a teenager fighting against my parents' wishes.

"You confuse me."

"You slay me, and I don't think I have ever felt what I do for you," I confess and lift my hand. "Don't ask me for a definition, June, I might never give it to you. This is who I am. I'm not broken, just forged in a different way than many, and I can promise to be loyal but never to fit in your mold."

She nods. "Let's give a chance to whatever is happening between us," she concludes. "So, besides our complicated relationship, what are we going to do with our spawns?"

I chuckle because the term isn't endearing but funny. I've never wanted children or a family. I've said it enough times. Until now. Fuck if I don't want to be with her for every step of the way. I can't wait to see her swollen belly, carrying my babies. Listen to their heartbeat, hold them when they come into the world. I want everything with her.

"Raise them together, no matter how things progress, we're in this together, baby," I answer, hoping she can read between the lines because it's obvious that me telling her that I can't live without her was not only confusing but too much to handle.

I don't regret setting my cards on the table. We're meant for each other. She just has to come to terms with it.

"Can we have breakfast?"

I reach out to her and kiss her knuckles. "How about an appetizer?" I ask, wiggling my eyebrows.

"Appetizer?" Her voice quivers with need, her eyes brighten with desire.

"Do you know how much you turn me on when you wear my shirts?" I pull her closer, caging her between my arms. "Let me eat you before I feed you."

"We shouldn't," she whispers.

"But we will," I say and slant my mouth on hers.

JUNE

❄

It was nine o'clock before we arrived home with my parents. Centennial Airport is only a twenty-minute drive from the house. The plan was to pick them up at four and bring them home where we'd have dinner. But just like it's been happening in the past few weeks, nothing has worked the way I plan it.

"The house is beautiful," Mom says as we enter. "The Christmas decorations are lovely. I think you could use a few more lights outside. Your dad could install them."

I look at Sterling and smile because I told him just that. The trees could use some twinkle lights and maybe we should hire someone to frame the house too. Sterling just rolls his eyes and mouths, *like mother like daughter*. I shrug.

Talking about Christmas and since Jackson hacked my evening with my parents, I suggest, "Maybe you can help me convince Jackson to spend Christmas Eve here. We have plenty of room for everyone."

She studies the place and looks at me. "It's Caroline and Marianne's first Christmas."

When she mentions the twins, I know I have to get on with the program and forget my amazing idea.

"Well, next year it's ours if we're going to follow *that* protocol," Sterling says and looks at my belly with a smile.

"Sounds like a good idea," I agree and glance at my parents nervously but neither one says a word.

"Why don't you follow me, Mr. and Mrs. Spearman?" Sterling says. "There're a few features I need to show you."

I sigh with relief. I'm not sure when we'll speak about the big elephant. Well, I don't look like one yet but I'm sure since I'm expecting two babies, I'll look like one soon. Still, are we discussing my pregnancy now or not until the kids turn eighteen?

When we picked up my parents neither one mentioned the subject. I assume it was because Jackson met us at the airport. We ended up going to his house for dinner.

Dad glares at Sterling when he grabs the bags and asks them to follow him. Actually, he's been glaring at my guy since he arrived. Okay, today isn't a good day to talk about the babies. I follow right behind. They're staying in the downstairs bedroom, far enough from the master suite.

Not that we're having sex. Not until I have a clear understanding of what we mean to each other. Morning sex in the kitchen was a little slip that I won't let happen again. I slipped because with that speech he gave me I was in a daze. It didn't let me think much. Tonight, it is different.

Because you're not horny now?

I admit, the desire is choking me. If I could, I'd drag him to the room and ask him to fuck me. Not that I can behave like that in front of my parents. I want them to like him.

So far, he's been a gentleman with my parents. Not that he's ever been rude. Actually, I had no idea what to expect from him until I saw him in action. He's polite with Dad and charming with Mom. I continue walking behind the three of them.

"Just place your finger on the scanner," Sterling says as he programs Dad's fingerprints on the alarm keypads.

"Is this necessary?" Dad asks as he watches Mom while she's following Sterling's instructions.

"We arm the alarm around ten o'clock at night and it doesn't disarm until six in the morning," he says. "If you need to leave the house before or after, you have access. Also, when we leave, we turn it on."

"This seems like a safe area, I don't feel like this is necessary," Dad protests.

"If you need anything, Beck and the team are available to help," Sterling continues. "June has a security detail."

"Is that necessary?" Dad insists, studying the house. "What are you, a drug dealer?"

"James," Mom says his name with a warning voice.

Dad glares at Sterling. "He has more bodyguards than a diplomat."

"He's had stalkers parading around his property," I explain, lying just a little because Sterling's stalkers sound dangerous and his fans intense. Then I add, "Like Alex."

"I don't like this." Dad pauses and looks at me. "I trust your judgment, but I don't have to like it, Junie."

"It's been a long day," Sterling speaks, taking my hand. "Please, make yourself at home, Mr. and Mrs. Spearman."

"I agree, James, let's go. Good night, Sterling. Junie."

"Good night, Mom," I say and walk to her open arms. Then I whisper, "Is Dad upset?"

"We'll talk tomorrow, Junie." She hugs me one more time and says loud enough for everyone to hear, "Just give him time, you're his baby."

I roll my eyes because things never change. Dad gives me a hug, kisses the top of my head, and nods toward Sterling.

"Hey, come with me," Sterling requests, pulling me toward the office.

"What are we doing?"

"Deactivating my social media accounts," he responds, taking his computer out of the case and setting it on top of the desk. "Should I write something on my website?"

"All of them?"

He nods once.

"After you're done, I'll type a news release or maybe just a quick note. Something simple and yet eloquent," I offer. "Maybe we can add one of your life changing quotes."

I pull out my phone and take a picture of him. "We'll post this with something like, time to step into a new chapter."

He smiles and kisses my cheek. "Thank you, I think that's genius. Now, tell me how to win your dad because nothing I did today was good enough."

"Stop trying so hard, he can smell bullshit," I say, laughing. "You heard Mom, I'm his baby. Be yourself, I don't think you realize how amazing you are, Sterling Ahern."

"There's nothing special about me." He sits on the chair and pulls me into his lap. "I'm a lucky bastard, because I found you, precious girl. You're who makes me want to be a better version of myself."

I close my eyes when he grips my hair to the side and his mouth kisses my exposed throat. The erotic way he grazes my skin makes me gasp. He then kisses my mouth and what seemed like a sweet tender moment becomes a desperate exchange.

His hungry mouth ravishes mine. I should be pushing him away because ... I can't remember why. He kisses me again and again, telling me how much he needs me. Our chemistry doesn't diminish, it strengthens as the days go by.

He anchors my hips against his hardness. I quiver as I beg him to fill me. "Please!"

I am overcome with desire and I sway my hips searching for release.

"June." I hear Dad calling me. "Where is she, Ari?"

"Let me go and check what they need," I say, rising from my seat. "We agreed to no sex, Mr. Ahern."

He gives me a mischievous smirk. "I just do what you ask, sweetheart. Your body was asking for it."

❄

THE NEXT MORNING, I wake up early, take a shower, and get ready to face my parents. Unfortunately, I forgot to let Mom know that the bacon makes me nauseous and as I enter the kitchen my stomach contracts violently. It's the plate of bacon and eggs on top of the counter.

I run to the powder room and barely make it on time. Seconds later, I feel Sterling's hand rubbing my back and he places a cold compress on my neck. "Sorry, baby. I asked your mom to start the kettle."

After the whole, washing face, brushing teeth, and taking a few deep breaths, I go back in the kitchen.

Sterling is already preparing my tea and oatmeal.

"She doesn't like oatmeal," Mom says.

"Surprisingly, I do now," I correct her.

"When are you due?" Mom asks. Dad sighs.

"August first," I answer, waiting for a congratulations or something nice. Neither one moves. "I'm having twins."

She nods, Dad fires a question, "Where are you going to live? In case you're interested, there are a couple of houses for sale in our neighborhood."

"I'm not going back to Sacramento. As you've heard last night, I'm selling the company. Jackson and I are discussing the possible buyers later today. Colorado seems like a nice state to raise children and they'll have Marianne and Caroline."

Sterling stands next to me. "I support her decisions. If she wants us to move to San Francisco, stay here in Colorado, or try another country. I'll follow her."

"What are your intentions with my daughter?" Dad asks and Sterling looks at me.

"Dad, not now," I say.

"Do you understand that the lives of two children are at stake and you don't want to talk about it? This isn't Facebook where you can check the option of it's complicated. I thought you were more responsible than this, Juniper. From all my children, you're the last one I'd think would be screwing with the future of her own children."

Sterling steps in front of me and says, "Before you judge, you should congratulate her. She's been wanting these children for a long time and she's finally reaching her dreams. With all due respect, sir, don't screw up your relationship with her because of society standards. June is more ready than anyone I've ever met. Our relationship has nothing to do with the future of our babies. They'll grow up loved with two loving parents. Now if you'll excuse me, I have work to do."

He turns around, kisses me, and leaves the house.

"What does that mean, June?" Mom asks.

I explain everything and once I'm done Dad hugs me and apologizes. "Sorry, I just don't want to see you hurt. It's so hard to not see you as a six-pound five-ounce baby who needs my protection."

"Congratulations, sweetie. I'm sorry for the inquisition but I'm worried you've been acting so strange and haven't confided in anyone."

I don't tell them Em and Hannah have been supporting me. "Look, I was going to do this one way or another. Instead of an anonymous donor, it happened with Sterling. He's a loving man and if you give him a chance—"

"Are you two together?" Dad asks.

I shake my head. "No, I'm not ready. He's giving me space; I hope you can respect it."

Dad's nostrils flare. Mom goes to his side and rubs his arm. "She's not a little girl, James. But she needs us, and we'll be beside her. You asked me what I wanted to do next year. I want to be with her."

"You don't have to, Mom, but if you guys want to stick around, I have plenty of room."

She smiles because usually I tell her off and send her to Alex or Jeannette who like to be babied.

"We'll find a place nearby. I'll ask Jackson or Jason to recommend us a realtor."

He opens his arms and I walk toward them.

"I had no idea you wanted this and I'm happy for you, sweetie. You know I'm going to love them and spoil them."

"Thank you, Mom and Dad."

This wasn't that bad, I'm not sure how Jackson is going to react, but I'll be ready for his outburst.

STERLING

Leaving June with her parents didn't settle well in the pit of my stomach. I had to do it. Plus I felt like an outsider and her dad was pissing me off. She's not a kid. Perhaps this is a normal reaction and I'm the one who was out of line.

She's not asking for anything. In fact, she has almost all her shit figured out. I'm the one variable in her life who is making her lose her cool.

The moment I arrive in my studio, I send her a text.

Sterling: *I hope that what I said didn't create a problem between you and your dad.*

June: *You were incredible, thank you.*

Sterling: *It was nothing.*

They needed to know how important this is to June. It's not an accident she's trying to fix but a dream she's able to fulfill and I'm fucking happy that she's letting me be a part of it.

June: *It was, see you soon?*

Sterling: *I'll be working for a few hours but come and visit if you dare. My table is anxious to have you—me too.*

June: *Is that a challenge, Mr. Ahern?*

Sterling: *Are you brave enough to accept it, Ms. Spearman?*
June: *Enjoy work xo*

I put my phone away and set up my materials. For a couple of hours, I work on a piece I want to give her for Christmas. But there's something that James Spearman said that keeps nagging me so first I text Abby apologizing for my behavior and promising to invite her to dinner soon. Then, I call Wes.

"This better be important," he answers immediately.

"Maybe not for you," I say. "Are you still in town?"

"For a couple of days," he answers, his voice serious, and I bet he's mad because of the way I behaved with Abby. "Are you ready to talk about June?"

He doesn't let me speak; he fires up the first question. Fuck, when is he going to let me work things at my own pace? Never, he's Wes fucking Ahern.

"She's different," I start.

"We gather that much. When something matters to you, you protect it with your life. You don't want us close to her yet," he explains. "Do you think I'm going to tell her what an asshole you used to be?"

"It's a lot more complicated than you think," I explain. "Everything between us is new. Plus, I'm trying to convince her that I'm worth sticking around."

"You are, but does she know about your baggage?"

I drum my fingers against the table. "Last night we closed my social media accounts. She understands me like no one else."

"I'm always here for you, slugger," he calls me by my ridiculous childhood name. "You're my brother and I've tried everything to include you into my family, but you keep pushing us away. There's just so fucking much I can take."

June's right. If I had asked or let them be there for me life wouldn't be so ... lonely. There, I accept it, I've been miserable and alone for the past couple of years. If she hadn't come into my life and brightened everything around me, I wouldn't have noticed it.

"It's not that I don't love you or want you around. But you're what I have left, and I couldn't forgive myself if one of my crazy fans hurt either one of you."

"You didn't give us a choice," he says almost the same words June did when I told her about the situation. "We love you, Sterling, and these couple of years have been hard for me. I thought we were past the bullshit and suddenly I lost you and then Mom."

"Sorry," I apologize. "I'm going to work harder because I want you to be part of my life. June is important and … we're expecting."

"Fuck, are you kidding me? You're expecting a baby," he says with an astonished voice. "She's my fucking hero."

"Twins," I add. "She's fucking amazing. Not sure why she appeared into my life because I'm the last person who deserves someone but she's still around. I'm so fucking afraid to mess everything up."

"You're more than our parents let you believe. Of course, you deserve someone brilliant and loving like you. You won't fuck things up, slugger, because when you love, you love with all your heart," he says and the excitement in his voice makes me want to believe that maybe June will accept me. "When do I get to meet her?"

"Soon, her family is in town. I don't want to overwhelm her."

"Wait, you're meeting the family?"

I whistle and tell him what's been happening the past couple of weeks. It feels so different and I'm relieved that I'm finally patching things up with him.

❋

BECK ENTERS the studio after knocking on the door. I check the clock and it's around noon. Fuck, where did the time go? I meant to text June to see if she wanted me to bring something or cook for her.

"You got a visitor," he says casually. "Randy will stay while I take my lunch break."

I frown, Randy stayed with June today. "Who is with June?"

He grunts some nonsense and opens the door wider. I smile like an idiot when I see my girl stepping into the room.

"Hello, gorgeous," I greet her.

"So here's where the magic happens," she says, looking everywhere. "Have you thought about cleaning up a little?"

"Stay away from my mess, Juniper," I warn her but smile because she could do whatever she wants with me and my studio. Mostly with me.

"I'm naked." She points at the sketches on the table. "Multiple times. I look like Jessica Rabbit here. I'm afraid my tits are never going to look like this."

Then she picks up another one. "This tattoo, it's lovely."

"You like it?"

She nods and turns her head, trying to look at her back, or her butt. "Maybe once the babies are older, we can do something smaller. I'm not sure I have the patience to stay still for hours until they're done with this masterpiece."

"I could paint it on you right now," I suggest. "Just take off your blouse and bend over my table."

She laughs and the vibrating sound stirs me up and makes me hard. This woman has a lot of power over me.

"You wish, Ahern."

"Of course, I do, baby. It's all I've been thinking about since ... I met you."

She shakes her head and hands me over a tote bag. "Here, I made us some sandwiches for lunch. You can tell me all about the places where you hide."

"There aren't many. I talked to my brother," I say, changing the subject.

"What's up with your relationship with him? Sometimes I feel like you're close, others that you hate him."

I shake my head and start my story from the beginning. "He was my parents' first foster kid. Almost a year after he arrived, I was born."

As we eat lunch, we discuss my parents. Dad's will. He left most of the company to Wes who hated the company as much as I did. By Wes's logic, if he has to deal with the legacy I do too, so we own it in equal parts now.

"Maybe our children would want to manage it or sell it," I offer. "We have a great team of executives in charge."

We talk some more about the properties I own and then she mentions her parents. "Mom and Dad might look into renting or buying a place."

"Pool house," I suggest. "They can stay in the pool house. If not, I have other houses."

"Thank you." She takes out another container from the tote bag she brought. "Dessert. I went to Like Home to buy a couple dozen macaroons. I met the owners, by the way, and I ordered lavender macaroons for this weekend. They're so good."

"This is whipped cream."

"Right." She grins mischievously. "This is for us to share. The cookies are just for me."

Licking her lips, she tells me, "Challenge accepted."

I set the container on my table and pull her to me. "I knew you had a wild side."

She places her palms on my chest. "Umm, nope, I am the one enjoying the whipped cream," she pauses, "on you."

June glides her hands down my torso and pulls the hem of my shirt. "We're changing the way you do things, Ahern. I call the shots during the day."

The throaty voice and the idea of her taking charge has my erection pressing painfully against my pants.

"Do you know what I want?" she asks when her fingers brush my erection through the denim fabric.

"Whatever it is, take it," I answer. "It's yours."

"Take off your shirt," she orders, and I obey.

She runs her fingers along my stomach. "I want to lick you and then swallow you."

I moan and close my eyes, almost coming in my pants as I imagine her on her knees between my legs. Her mouth taking me slowly, drawing me deep until I hit the back of her throat.

"You want my mouth, Sterling?" she asks seductively.

"You're going to pay for this tonight," I warn her and the smile playing on her face makes me shiver. "I'm talking blindfolds and ice cream."

"You talk a lot, let's see who wins this match," she says, running a wandering hand across my stomach and unfastening my jeans. My length springs, ready to fuck her mouth. She moves my pants farther down and as she kneels in front of me her tongue traces the lines of my muscles and then, she kisses my tip.

I jolt, and she smirks.

"If you last long enough, I'll let you bend me over." She pauses, biting her lip. "If not, I get to boss you around tonight."

"What happened to no sex, minx?"

She opens her mouth wide and licks around the base, nipping my sack. "You challenged me; I can't walk away. It becomes personal."

She sucks my tip and lowers her mouth oh so slowly, I'm having trouble controlling myself. Fuck, if she wins this round what's she going to do with me tonight?

JUNE

On my drive to Jack's office, I keep thinking about lunch. And the time Sterling and I spent together. I'm not sure where I gathered the courage to walk into his studio and just take charge, but I loved every second of it. I loved it more when he held me close and said, "You're the best thing that's happened in my life, there's not even a close second."

When I park the car, I close my eyes momentarily to savor the peaceful moment we shared before I had to leave his studio.

There're so many things that scare me about this guy. The way we fit so well, how easily we can go from a serious conversation to mind-blowing sex and then comfortable silence. How well he reads me when he barely knows me. The way I get lost in us. It makes me uneasy how fast we've come to settle into a relationship. Also, that he doesn't like titles or permanency.

I grab my things. It's time to face Jackson Spearman, and the guy is going to try to bulldoze me into a plan where I do things his way so I can have a "better" life.

"He's in his office waiting for you," his assistant says when I arrive.

"Thank you," I reply and swing the door open meeting my fate.

"What is he doing here?" I ask when I spot Jason. A second later, Alex comes out of the private bathroom.

"Great, three Spearmans!" I growl.

"You're selling my career to some idiot," Alex protests. "I have the right to be here."

"No, I'm taking you with me. I won't leave you, now go away," I argue.

He leans against the wall and crosses his arms. "Still, I'm staying."

"And you?" I turn to Jason.

He shrugs. "I might know someone who wants to buy it."

"Well, since almost everyone knows, let's get this over with then you two have to leave." I rub my temples and say out loud. "I'm pregnant."

Jackson says, "I fucking knew it. I'm going to kill that asshole."

"Seriously, you're going to start with that line, Jackson Spearman? Cool it and listen to me because I'm not going to tolerate nonsense. This pregnancy was bound to happen. I planned it. Actually, I had *everything* planned to get knocked up this year."

"By him?"

I look up at the ceiling and take a deep cleansing breath. He's so smart but sometimes he can be such an idiot.

"No, Jack, I was going through artificial insemination. If that didn't work, the next step was IVF. I wanted a baby and for some crazy reason things worked out differently than I planned."

Straightening my shoulders and glancing at the three of them, I speak calmly. "I'm thirty-three. It'd be nice to be treated like an adult. It's exhausting to be me. I have to show you guys that I'm old enough to live my own life. It's getting old."

I set my things on his desk. "Who took care of you when you were going through your divorce, Jackson? And when things weren't working out with Emmeline? I took a week off and came to stay with you."

I don't add that Jeannette was with me, the point is that we're always taking care of them.

Then, I switch my attention to Jason. "Or who looked after you when that bitch abandoned you at the altar?"

Alex lifts his hands. "I know, you take care of me all the time. When Nikki, Charlotte, Edna, Kelly, and the others left me. Or when I was in that car accident, and you took care of everything."

"So what do I have to do so you can understand I'm not a baby?"

Jackson smirks. "Aw, but you'll always be the baby of the family, Junie."

I growl.

Jackson presses his lips together and sighs. "Why didn't you tell me all this before?"

"Because what's the point? You'd have tried to convince me not to do it," I answer. "The only two people who I confided in were Em and Hannah because they are one hundred percent behind me and not wondering if I'm old enough to do stuff."

He runs a hand through his hair and takes a deep breath. "What do you need from me?"

I'm astounded by his calm tone. "What?"

"I don't want to lose you. My only options are to change or see you during the holidays. I will change," he offers. And then he surprises me by saying, "Congratulations on the baby."

"Well, not to brag or say, I can too but they're twins." I smirk.

Jason laughs and walks to me to hug me tight. "Some things don't change, you had to compete with Jack. When is your due date?"

"The first week of August."

Jack and Alex hug me too and it's nice to know that they can listen and see me as their equal.

"Look, June, I love you and I support you. This is all good and I'm sure you'll rock the motherhood shit just like you rock everything in the world. But ..." Jason pauses, giving me one of those, this is for your own good looks. "Ahern isn't what you need."

"Stop right there," I order, lifting my hand. "My relationship with him isn't any of your business. We're getting to know each other but we both agree that parenting the babies matters the most. I'll decide if he's good for me. Who knows, maybe I'm not good for him."

"Now can we discuss my company?"

JUNE

I SAVOR THE DAYS THAT LEAD INTO CHRISTMAS, EVERYTHING SEEMS normal. By normal I mean, morning sickness, meetings with potential buyers and current clients. So much for I'm taking the month of December off. Fortunately, at night when the door of my bedroom closes, I have Sterling to make everything worth it.

Spending every available moment we have is our number one priority. He's getting ready for next year's exhibition. We're going to Paris and staying there for a month. I'm beyond excited. This is the first time I'll travel with the guy I'm dating. Not that we have a relationship status, yet.

It doesn't matter. I never thought I'd become so familiar with someone so quickly. We've learned each other's expressions, meals, words … He might be easygoing but I've learned he has a big temper and knows how to keep it under control. He's a tease and likes to experiment in bed. We both do.

He's also sweet. So sweet he's tried to make this Christmas special, if not the best for both of us.

Jeannette arrives later today. She convinced Teagan to spend Christmas Eve with us and Christmas day with her parents. Sterling is paying for the trips. I think he likes me. I'm getting used to the domestic life we're settling into. We haven't talked about the future but I want to talk about it now.

My parents are with Jackson today. Dad's playing Santa. Not that Caroline and Marianne will understand it, but I can't wait to see the pictures from the photo shoot.

I'm in the living room waiting for Sterling to finish his conversation with Beck. Apparently, someone is looking for him and whoever it is needs some kind of clearance to speak with Sterling or it's a business that needs his attention. I didn't understand the code well.

Until now, I had no idea they had codes. I hug myself tight because what if there's a stalker or—

No, don't let your imagination or yesterday's bad thriller get the best of you.

Maybe think about how you're going to surprise Sterling with his present. Mom helped me make it. What can you give a guy who has everything? I wonder if he's going to like the onesies and his matching T-shirt. Just then he saunters into the room, red face, flaring nostrils, and papers in hand.

"What in the fucking hell, Juniper?" he yells, slamming a manila envelope on the table. All the papers he is holding fall to the floor. "At least have the fucking courage to tell me this in person."

I frown and pick up one of the pages on the floor. It's a memo, from my lawyer and ... I cover my mouth. Did I forget to call him? I close my eyes momentarily trying to remember what happened. I exchanged emails with my lawyer and cleaned the kitchen. Then Sterling barged in the house, we talked, had sex ...

My brain stops working when Sterling sexes me up and leaves me in a daze of desire.

"Sterling, let me explain," I say.

"You and these children have become the axis on which my entire world spins and what do you do ... on Christmas Eve?" He laughs and the sound is empty, angry. "Merry Fucking Christmas,

Sterling Ahern. This is what I think about handing me your heart." He rakes his hair. "For once in my life I let myself enjoy the near-magical quality of the holidays. It's all a trick. Nothing was real."

"Sterling—"

He dusts his hands. "Look, you don't want to be with me, I get it. It fucking hurts but I won't force you to it. You played along and got a good fuck while it was fun. I should've seen it when you were spending so much time trying to figure out your future and pushing away your hiatus. You made a decision."

My eyes sting, he's hurting so much, and I am the one who hurt him. How am I going to fix it? It feels as if he has built a wall of steel between us and I've lost him. This can't be happening. Not today—or ever.

"It's not what you think," I say, but he's not listening.

"I'm not stupid. My reading level is high enough to understand what those papers mean and what you're trying to accomplish. I might spend my entire day creating art but I can run a company, Juniper. I guess you don't get how much power I have, but I'll be happy to show you. I scanned the papers and sent them to my lawyer. You'll receive a counter in a few days."

He turns around and leaves me standing still.

❄

STERLING'S STANDING in the shower, hands flat on the tile wall. His head bent, the water washing him down. He's pissed off at me. I'm not sure if what I have to say and what I bring will be enough to earn his trust.

Old me would just turn around and leave, back to San Francisco where nothing touches me, feelings don't happen, and I have built a life that's safe.

But I don't want any of that, *I want us.*

"The day after we came back from Steamboat, when you didn't

come to dinner. That's when I emailed my lawyer. I forgot all about it until ... now."

"We have nothing to talk about, June," he says with a warning. He glares at me, jaw clenched, water running down his body. "If you're trying to talk to me so I don't take the children away from you, I won't. I'm just going to make sure I have daily access to them. This will be their house. We'll share custody."

"Hear me out, you can believe me or not. You said it once. We talk everything out, no bullshit. It was a mistake," I confess, hating to admit that I make more mistakes than everyone else around me. I just know how to cover them up well.

"You don't make mistakes, June," he says sharply and turns around facing the wall. "Leave."

I step into the shower. The water slips into my clothes. My face is soaked, washing away the tears that are finally rolling down my cheeks.

"Why do you think I have a routine and I write everything down? To avoid mistakes and surprises. Still, they happen more often than you can imagine. I cover them well. I'm an expert. Only Jeannette and Hannah know how much I fuck up, but I hate being less than perfect. I only let people see my success. So yeah, I screw up more often than many."

He finally turns around, lifts my chin, and looks into my eyes. "Why did you do it?"

"I was just trying to get ahead of the game because I thought you were done with me and ... I kept telling myself this was to protect *them*, but I was protecting my heart because I was already falling in love with you. Never in my life had I ever felt so alive and that I could finally be myself. If you signed the papers, I wouldn't have to hear my heart shattering every time you rejected *me*.

"We talked the next morning, and you confused me in so many ways. But you said you were mine. That meant everything to me. I just had no idea how to keep you and not crowd you. Someone like you wouldn't want to be trapped. So, I've been too busy thinking about us and learning how to make a life with you. Trying to enjoy the moment and not focus on every single detail that used to dictate my life."

I laugh and crying harder because I don't know what else to say to make him stay.

"You make me feel things I have never felt before. Not only love, but a feeling of belonging—to you. Even when you're handsome and have wild bedroom eyes and an old soul that stirs everything inside me, I love that you're spontaneous, thoughtful, and caring."

"You love me," he whispers.

"Of course, it's easy to fall in love with you," I mumble. "You're so intense... and who wouldn't fall for you, Sterling? Hear me out, I would never take the babies away from you, even when what you feel for me disappears someday."

"Never," he says, kissing my temple and embracing me. "You're the big love that I never expected. The blizzard brought you to me. You're a fucking storm with high winds, destroying my walls. You heat my cold heart and slowly have molded me into someone new. If you ever leave me, I'll be an incomplete piece of clay. Finish me, make me the man you deserve by just being with me."

STERLING

❄

WE SPEND CHRISTMAS EVE IN THE HOUSE. AROUND MIDNIGHT, when everyone who stayed with us goes to their bedrooms, I get ready for tonight's surprise. Christmas is just a few minutes away.

"Do you trust me?" I ask June as we reach the bottom of the stairs.

"Blindly," she responds and smiles because I pull out a blindfold. "What are you doing?"

"Humor me," I say, covering her eyes.

Slowly, we make our way to the upstairs area. "I'm going to trip," June complains. "This is silly."

"Just admit you hate surprises," I say, guiding her toward the room and stopping right in the middle of the hallway where I press the switch to turn on the twinkle lights I had installed while she was shopping with her mom during the weekend.

Jason and Alex came through, I asked them to sprinkle pinecones and snowflake shaped confetti before they went to their rooms.

"Okay, you can uncover your eyes now," I say.

She has the biggest smile I've ever seen in my entire life.

"This is a lot of holiday cheer for ol' Scrooge," she jokes. "But so beautiful."

I guide her to our bedroom and when she opens the door, she gasps. "We have a tree."

She tosses her arms around me and hugs me. "When did you do this?"

"Merry Christmas," I whisper into her ear and release her. "It's time to open your presents."

She walks to the tree that sits in her reading nook, then she turns back and says, "Why are your presents here too?"

"Your mom said I should bring those three with me just in case," I explain, marching toward her.

I bend and give her the first one.

"These are beautiful," she says, pulling the ornaments out of the tissue paper. "Baby's first Christmas."

I made them for her, for our babies. Two snowflakes, they're similar but not the same.

She looks up at me, her eyes glistening with tears that she's about to shed. "They're perfect."

I pick up the next present. This time she shreds the wrapping paper and smiles at the ornament of two tangled snowflakes. "Our first Christmas."

"How did you know I'd love this? They're my favorite ornaments."

I gather her into my chest, kissing her. "You're my favorite. Everything about you is what gives me joy. I couldn't ask for a better present or a better life."

Brushing a kiss against her lips, I pull out the velvet box and drop to one knee.

"Sterling," she says my name with fear in her voice. "No, you don't have to."

"I know, but I want to with all my heart." I slide the ring onto her finger. It fits just perfect. "Have I mentioned that as an artist I observe and learn more than people give me credit for?"

She nods slowly.

"I learned to trust you with my heart, that the only reason I've never found love is because I hadn't met you. For this relationship to work, I have to give you everything without expecting anything back. I'm afraid enough to have the courage to ask you to be mine forever. I can't live without you."

"I love you so much, Sterling Ahern. I never thought this much happiness could be within my reach. That I would fall so madly in love so fast and feel so ... alive. I can't live without you either," she confesses and begins to cry.

"Don't cry, beautiful girl." I rise up and hug her. "You're never going to lose me. I'm yours forever."

"You and our babies are the best Christmas present I could've ever asked for, I just can't believe it's actually happening."

I kiss her until her arms are twined around my neck.

"We're in this for the long run, right?"

"Yes, we are," she says.

My heart jackhammers against my rib cage, yet I'm filled with a sense of righteous calmness I've never had in my life. We're enough to make each other happy. This isn't contentment, it's happiness and a sense of fulfillment. My heart is finally full.

I sway her against my body as we stare at the Christmas tree and the nativity set I made for her. The last few days I've spent my time in the studio creating what I thought would bring a smile. Maybe in fifty years we'll be decorating for our grandchildren with these same ornaments and wouldn't it be amazing to tell them the story of how the most wonderful woman in the world taught me that love really exists.

"I love you," I whisper. "With all my heart."

EPILOGUE

Sterling

A Year Later ...

June hated surprises. Her life is full of them. That was until her twelve-week checkup. The doctor recommended a second sonogram. Her belly was bigger than the gestational age of the babies. Surprise, they didn't detect the third fetus during the first sonogram.

There's a joke going around about Jack and Em trying to have quadruplets to outdo us.

Our time together has been full of surprises and we are ready for more.

We married in February, in France at a cute château in Midi-Pyrenees. It was an intimate ceremony. We celebrated with our families and our closest friends.

In mid-July, our babies arrived. Violet, Vaughn, and Vanessa. Like their mom, they stole my heart the moment I held them.

James and Aria live close by, but some nights they stay in the guest room to help us. Raising our babies is a team effort.

However, they also spend time with Marianne, Caroline, and Blake, Jason's son.

Wes and Abby visit us often and have been embraced by the Spearman family too. We're so close that the entire family spent Thanksgiving in Tahoe. My brother hosted it and Ari helped organize everything.

I can't remember how life was before June and her family came into my life. She changed everything, including my priorities.

This year the house is the North Pole. I bet Santa might want to copy the light design Wes helped me create.

Our little ones turned five months old a couple of weeks ago. They came to change my life, teach me more than I've learned through my travels, and keep me awake all fucking night. But I adore them.

"God, I don't think I'm going to stay awake for long," June mumbles, biting her lip. "What are we having for dinner?"

I laugh and stare at her.

"Stop staring like that, your son is eating and you're thinking about s-e-x."

"Lucky baby." I bend, securing the girls who are sleeping in my arms, and kiss her. "Let me set the princesses in their crib. I'll help you with him once you're done. Maybe we can whip something up if you really don't want to go to Jack's tonight."

She shakes her head. "It's okay. We can't skip it. I'm just tired. Hooray for teething."

June laughs and I join. We're bone-tired but I don't think we'd do anything differently. Maybe how we celebrate this year.

We split the holiday. Christmas Eve is at Jack's, breakfast at Jason's, and we have dinner tomorrow in the house. June has everything ready for tomorrow, including catering. She's learned that with three kids, it's best if she just uses her resources instead of trying to look like a superstar. She is a superstar, I'm just proud of her for learning to enjoy what matters.

"Remind me to only have one kid the next time you knock me up," she says and I freeze.

"What did you say?"

She shrugs. "Wouldn't it be nice to have a couple more babies?"

"You SOB, this is all your fault. I'm never having s-e-x with you," I repeat the words she said during labor and smirk. "So far you've broken the no touching you rule—several times. And now we want another one."

"Not now," she says, as if that makes it different. "Later, in a couple of years. It'll be like my brothers and us. We are so close that we are best friends."

I shake my head and take Vaughn from her arms, set him on the left side of my chest, snuggling him close to me, smoothing his back. When I fell in love with June, I never knew it could be such a strong feeling that could overpower anything. My kids though, they taught me that the love I have for their mother is nothing compared to what I feel for them.

My biggest hope is that I can be a good father to them. That we can become friends and they can come to me for anything.

June keeps telling me how I have to let the fear of being my father go and just enjoy my relationship with our kids. She's right and I'm working hard to be who they need and not what I wanted my father to be for me.

"Let's take a nap," I suggest as I set my son in the crib.

When I turn around, she's looking at me. My breath still catches when I see her. She's beautiful, sexy, and mine. The best present I've ever received in my entire life.

Happy Holidays!

Thank you so much for reading Once Upon a Holiday. Writing it was as much fun. So here's a behind the scenes story about this book.

Originally, I was done writing for the year but as I try to plot and write my first release for 2020, there's this story just wanting to be told. June Spearman didn't want to wait until next year. Why would she when her older brothersealready had their story?

Everything just fell into place. Sterling and I have been going back and forth about his story. It was supposed to be a second chance romance, but I just couldn't picture him going back to Kara. With a simple glance I realize these two were meant to be together.

Plotting the story was easy, the beginning was a little rough. I wanted it angsty.

Karen, my PA made sure I understood the definition of Holiday cheer because if you've read me before I can get pretty angsty. So, I said, "what if they meet when she enters the wrong restroom?"

I wasn't there to see her—not even on the phone to hear her. However, I imagine she laughed for hours. The same way she laughed back in April when we had dinner after Talkbooks Author Event. Because of course things like that not only happen to June but also to me.

Closing such a fun year with this book feels just right. Next year, you'll have Alex's story. His story has been plotted. It's fun, different and as usual he has a leading lady that will have him trembling and wanting for a lot more.

If you like this book, I'd appreciate if you could write a review on Amazon; and recommend it to your friends. As an author, my visibility depends on you, my friend and your reviews.

Please, don't be a stranger, check my other books and visit my website where you can find all the social media places you can stalk me.

May the joy and peace of the holidays be with you all through the New Year. Wishing you a season of blessings.

Love,

Claudia xoxo

ACKNOWLEDGMENTS

This book is to celebrate the holidays, the magic of family, friends and everything that really matters.

Let me start with thanking Emery Jacobs for her medical advice. She listened to me for hours as I explained what I wanted for this story, and she helped me getting everything right. To my sister in-law who had to go through a similar procedure to have her twins. She walked me through her emotional journey.

I have so many people to thank, please forgive me if I forget to mention you. Know that you're important to me.

Without any order I have to start with Karen who is the best listener in the world, and is trying to keep me Mrs. Distraction organized. I can't say how wonderful is to have her as part of my team.

To my family. The husband who puts up with my crazy schedule, makes sure to feed me because he's a better cook, and loves me unconditionally.

Hang Le, thank you so much for this cover. I know we went back and forth a lot but we found the perfect fit!!

My gratitude goes to my girls who are incredible, Yolanda,

Melissa, and Patricia. They still put up with me, even when I flake big time!

To my editors, thank you so much!

My instagrammers, I have the most amazing Bookstagrammers and supporters. Ladies you're the best. Darlene, Chole, Amy ... the list is long and these women are fabulous.

Thank you to all the bloggers who help spread the word about my books. Ladies, this release was hard but your messages, your support and friendship kept me going. Though, I guess thank you doesn't cut it, your energy and support are what makes every release a success. Love you all.

My amazing ARC team, you ladies rock. Thank you for you patient and support.

To the Book Lovin' Chicas group, thank you so much for your continuous support. For your daily cheers, and the words of encouragement. I'm grateful for you.

To you, my readers. I am grateful to you. Thank you for reading my words, and for supporting my books. Thank you so much for those emails and notes, they mean so much to me.

Last but most importantly, I'd like to thank God for all the blessings in my life.

Love,
Claudia xoxo

ABOUT THE AUTHOR

Claudia is an award-winning, *USA Today* bestselling author. She lives in Colorado, working for a small IT. She has three children and manages a chaotic household of two confused dogs, and a wonderful husband who shares her love of all things geek. To survive she works continually to find purpose for the voices flitting through her head, plus she consumes high quantities of chocolate to keep the last threads of sanity intact.

To find more about Claudia:
 website
 Sign up for her newsletter: News Letter

Printed in Great Britain
by Amazon